VANITY*fair*

Inspiration for the look of the movie came from
diverse sources, including *Liverpool Quay by
Moonlight*, by John Atkinson Grimshaw, 1887.

Bringing Thackeray's Timeless Novel to the Screen

VANITY *fair*

A Mira Nair Film

Journals and Correspondence by *Mira Nair*

Screenplay by *Matthew Faulk & Mark Skeet*
and Julian Fellowes

NEWMARKET PRESS • NEW YORK

A NEWMARKET PICTORIAL MOVIEBOOK

This book is published in the United States of America.

First Edition

10 9 8 7 6 5 4 3 2 1   10 9 8 7 6 5 4 3 2 1
1-55704-637-9 (Paperback)   1-55704-638-7 (Hardcover)

Library of Congress Cataloging-in-Publication Data
available upon request.

QUANTITY PURCHASES
Companies, professional groups, clubs, and other organizations
may qualify for special terms when ordering quantities of this title.
For information, write Special Sales Department, Newmarket Press,
18 East 48th Street, New York, NY 10017; call (212) 832-3575;
fax (212) 832-3629; or e-mail mailbox@newmarketpress.com

www.newmarketpress.com

Edited by Linda Sunshine   Designed by Timothy Shaner

Manufactured in the United States of America.

Other Newmarket Pictorial Moviebooks include:
Two Brothers: A Fable on Film and How It Was Told
Van Helsing: The Making of the Legend
The Alamo: The Illustrated Story of the Epic Film
Cold Mountain: The Journey from Book to Film
In America: A Portrait of the Film
The Hulk: The Illustrated Screenplay
The Art of X2: The Collector's Edition
Gods and Generals: The Illustrated Story of the Epic Civil War Film
Chicago: From Stage to Screen—The Movie and Illustrated Lyrics
Catch Me If You Can: The Film and the Filmmakers
Frida: Bringing Frida Kahlo's Life and Art to Film
E.T. The Extra-Terrestrial: From Concept to Classic
*Windtalkers: The Making of the Film about the Navajo Code Talkers
of World War II*
Ali: The Movie and the Man
Planet of the Apes: Re-imagined by Tim Burton
*Moulin Rouge: The Splendid Book That Charts the Journey of Baz
Luhrmann's Motion Picture*
The Art of The Matrix
Gladiator: The Making of the Ridley Scott Epic
Crouching Tiger, Hidden Dragon: A Portrait of the Ang Lee Film
*The Age of Innocence: A Portrait of the Film Based on the
Novel by Edith Wharton*

Contents

For our beloved Mary Selway

1936–2004

Whose bravery and elegance blessed this film

LEFT: Image from the opening credits of *Vanity Fair*. ABOVE: Photo by Liane Harris.

Journals and Correspondence

by Mira Nair

William Makepeace Thackeray was born in Calcutta, the son of a collector in the service of the East India Company. His novel *Vanity Fair*, subtitled "A Novel Without a Hero," was published in monthly installments beginning in 1847 to the scandalized delight of Georgian society. In the novel, no infirmity of English society escaped his roving eye. Every hypocrisy, materialistic impulse, and social presumption is gleefully laid bare. At the novel's center is the lovely and cunning Miss Rebecca Sharp, one of the most memorable stars in the firmament of English literature and about whom Thackeray had clearly mixed intentions. Becky is the orphaned daughter of an impoverished London painter. At boarding school, she befriends the good, dear, and somewhat simpering Amelia Sedley and sets her hat on Amelia's brother Jos—who has done quite well for himself in India—to avert a future as a governess. In this design Becky is thwarted by Amelia's beloved, the callow young George Osborne, the indulged soldier son of a wealthy tradesman, who had not quite grasped the social rung his father imagined he paid for. Undaunted, Becky quickly retools and manages instead a secret match with Rawdon Crawley, the younger son of her employer Sir Pitt Crawley, and favored nephew to Tilly Crawley, a tyrannical unmarried dowager of means. Amelia, meanwhile, suffers a reversal of fortune and it is only through the remonstrances of George's good friend, Dobbin, who is himself in love with Amelia, that her devotion to the arrogant George is rewarded in marriage. This is, of course, a mere preamble to a novel that has a cast of hundreds, numerous battles and balls, a time-span of almost four decades, and a saga that begged for the kind of filmmaking that I half-jokingly called *Gone with the Vindaloo*. Such a novel does not submit to the medium of cinema without a struggle. Focus Features—the specialty films unit of NBC Universal—had a script by Matthew Faulk and Mark Skeet that had been in the works for nearly a decade. They offered me the film after the success of my last film, *Monsoon Wedding*, which they distributed. I was immediately interested—*Vanity Fair* had been one of my favorite novels from my Irish Catholic boarding school days in Simla in India—I remembered the interwoven stories of Becky and Amelia as a sort of nineteenth-century *Mean Girls*. With

What I love about *Vanity Fair* is that the chief character is the world; this lends itself to my particular carnivalesque sensibility. —Mira Nair

soul. I went home to Kampala, Uganda, for the summer, bringing books about Thackeray and Georgian England with me. I did my homework like a schoolgirl, coming up with a map of the world I wanted to create.

Upon re-reading the novel in the peace of my tropical garden, what I loved about it most was that the chief character was the world. This is what lent itself to my particular carnivalesque sensibility, and what I wished to heighten in the film. I admired Focus' existing script by Skeet and Faulk, and yet, as is typical when a director comes onto a project, there were some changes I wanted to make. I wanted to bring it closer to the democratic swirl of the multilayered book. I wanted to restore the role of Dobbin as the moral center of the story, and wanted a prominent love story between Becky and Rawdon, a governess and a gambler, who recognized the rascal in each other. I saw them as an earlier avatar of Bonnie and Clyde. I wanted the script to have a greater balance in the interrelatedness of the characters, thereby capturing the philosophy inherent in the book and what I call the yogic question Thackeray posed: "Which of us is happy in this world? Which of us has his desire? Or, having it, is satisfied?"

* * * * *

RIGHT: Director Mira Nair and screenwriter Julian Fellowes. LEFT: Rawdon Crawley (James Purefoy) welcomes Becky Sharp (Reese Witherspoon) to London.

Journals and Correspondence

I had known Reese Witherspoon before I approached her with *Vanity Fair*. I had never forgotten the stillness of her 10-year-old gaze in *The Man in the Moon*, and had marveled at her performance in *Election*. Her comic turn in *Legally Blonde* was equally brilliant, and we had talked about collaborating on a variety of projects. She was my first and only choice for playing Becky Sharp, one of the greatest female characters written in literature. Reese has wit, intelligence, guile, and that enticing quality called Appeal, which makes an actor a movie star. Becky is a complicated character; I wanted to preserve her complexity, her ambition, her folly, yet work with an actor like Reese who is just plain irresistible to watch. It's no fun seeing a movie where you hate the protagonist. Besides, if Reese played Becky, I knew young audiences in America would discover Becky Sharp—and my schoolgirl love for this great banquet of a novel would come full circle.

The first and only writer I thought of to make my vision come to life was Julian Fellowes, a true-blue toff and recent Oscar-winner for his lively and astute screenplay for *Gosford Park*. Luckily for me, Donna Gigliotti, one of the producers of the film, introduced him to me over high tea at Claridge's, and I found in him an equally helpless fan of Thackeray. Despite the fact that he was just about to begin his directing debut for his film, *A Way Through the Woods*, Julian cleared his plate for some weeks and became mine. And Thackeray's. We met on Labor Day weekend in my apartment in New York and immersed ourselves in Thackeray's clamorous world of social upheaval.

Subj: Thank You
Date: 9/5/2002 9:07:31 PM E. Africa Standard Time
From: Julian Fellowes
To: Mira Nair

Dearest Mira,

Left alone as we were, on holiday from our loved ones, I began to feel we were living a film starring George Peppard and Audrey Hepburn as we talked and ate and watched our movies and visited our delicious restaurants. I was describing it all to Emma and she listened and asked rather quizzically: "Yes, but did you get any work done?" But the truth is I feel we got an enormous amount of work done. We seem to share a vision of this film. It is not, for once, to be a tired, reverential revisit to an old classic nor an angry, make-it-modern, f*** you, punch in the face but a big, rich, intriguing tale which will make them laugh and use up several handkerchiefs—the ultimate movie experience. I am thrilled. Now of course I must get down to the work.

Subj: India?
Date: 9/19/2002 12:39:28 AM E. Africa Standard Time
From: Mira Nair
To: Julian Fellowes

Dear Julian,

Hoping it's all going clickety-clack.

I'm trying to make a case for shooting a few scenes in India because I think it will open up the film a whole lot: a fab change of place and light for us to truly understand the impact of the colonies, how far away and utterly different it was from England, etc. . . . I was thinking specifically of South India, where the landscape is wild and dense, and the inhabitants very dark and short ("native-looking"!) I've thought a bit about Dobbin—he was so much the moral center of the book, and I want to restore him to his rightful place in our story. To give him some physical "manly" action to do, what do you think about Amelia's letter being brought to Dobbin while he's on a palatial houseboat in the backwaters of Kerala (very lush, paddy and rubber plantations all around, an immediate shorthand of how different it is from England), he reads the letter, and in a mad rush jumps off the boat—with his clothes on—swimming to the banks, where Major and Mrs. Dowd are in the midst of a pukka English tea party to state his case like a love-soaked madman. . . ?

Much love, Mira

Subj: Re: India?
Date: 9/19/2002 8:23:33 PM E. Africa Standard Time
From: Julian Fellowes
To: Mira Nair

Dear Mira,

As for the scenes in India, I would vastly prefer them to be filmed there if they will go for it. That same old palm tree and man-in-a-tent with cicadas going in the background always tells you so clearly that the whole thing was shot in Surrey. . . . I don't see why we can't indicate them in a scene like the one you describe where Dobbin gets the letter congratulating him on his engagement. Why shouldn't he have to do something like swim ashore? I think we can make it sufficiently believable that he would do so. I like the idea of him actually "doing" something to try to get back to her. He is already sewn through the story much more than he was and is now an un-ridiculous figure which I am certain is right to make Amelia's fate satisfactory in movie terms.

MN: My idea of shooting a number of scenes in India did not fit within our budget. It was going to have to be Elveden for Bikaner, Gloucester for Rajasthan.

Subj: Dobbin
Date: 10/2/2002 8:09:34 PM E. Africa Standard Time
From: Julian Fellowes
To: Mira Nair

Dear Mira,

I am approaching the unveiling…

My own feeling about Dobbin is that, as we discussed, we have now traced his constant protection of Amelia much more thoroughly. We witness his realisation that Amelia will crack up if George abandons her (George's motives incidentally in marrying her are now, I think, clear. He acts in anger at his father's high-handedness and instantly regrets it). We see Dobbin suffering for Amelia when she's giving birth etc., etc., and if the actor is a gentlemanly and diffident hunk, as opposed to the usual goofy nonentity, then the audience will accept him as their moral guide and Amelia's proper romantic fate. I think he should be less showy and glamorous than George but NO less attractive in a growing-on-you sort of way. Do you agree?

I will try to telephone but I am on the run at the moment as I am obliged to attend my own farewell dinner up here and I set off at dawn to drive the length of Britain in one day.

From: Mira Nair
To: Julian Fellowes
Sent: Wednesday, October 02, 2002 9:28 AM
Subject: Re: VF

dear JF, am in London missing you but seeing all the hunks today. i see what you're saying about dobbin—leave it out for the moment, I think. The important thing is to realize that he was always Amelia's protector from afar, and I'm sure you've found a way to make that very clear. Dying to see the unveiling.

Much love, bon courage Mira

From: Mira Nair
To: Julian Fellowes
Sent: Tuesday, October 08, 2002 4:35 AM
Subject: Salaams for your Lovely Script

Dearest Julian, I hope you've forgiven me for not responding immediately to the unveiling of your marvellous work. I was given the script en route the airport, spent many hours enjoying it, and then returned to NY, staggering with jetlag and fatigue, to an enormous family reunion of sorts at home this weekend—so forgive the delay in writing you. I think you've done it again—the script has your inimitable rhythm and humour, and a great flow. All the relationships, the power play, the hypocrisy vs. the reality, are MUCH clearer. You have constructed a brilliant, and clearly distilled, tapestry of Thackeray's world. Now all I wish for is for certain lines to be funnier, more tart; AND for certain scenes to feel more emotional. As prom-

LEFT: The Indian casting director, Loveleen Tandan, found these bewitching child performers in Rajasthan to lead the magnificent finale of the film. Photo by Milan Moudgill.

ised, before I circulate the script to all concerned, I wanted to give you some li'l-bitty notes of mine to be incorporated:

1. Pg. 4: Thought Becky's French retort could be spicier. Far prefer it to the old line, but perhaps a little more bite?

2. LOVE SIR PITT (Met James Broadbent, who will be divine in the part, although I'm tempted to also consider him for Mr. Osborne—not because he's better for that, only because it's a bigger part and we can get to see him more.)

3. Pg. 34: I miss some friendly exchange between Becky and Amelia before the Becky-George interaction; after all, they haven't met in ages, etc., I LOVE BECKY'S PUTDOWN OF GEORGE...OOOH.

4. Pg. 45: Felt strongly that the piano should be delivered during the scene in which Dobbin comes to see Amelia. AND that the scene should be moved to the exterior for this (we have to be careful about how many interiors there are in this film). Also felt that Amelia's anguish re: George has to be more heightened in this scene to fuel Dobbin to go to George in the next scene to tell him "she's dying." Must say, I do miss the line in the book that Dobbin has when describing Amelia to G: I tell you, George, she's dying.

5. Pg. 64: While I like Rawdon's bluff manner in general, I wish for a little more tenderness in this parting scene before Waterloo. Gotta say I love the line from the book as he caresses her in farewell: "I may live to vex you yet." This scene could be more emotional than it reads presently.

6. Love the scene when Becky chooses to be with Amelia instead of leave Brussels. Julian, my eyes are closing—'tis late— may I send you the remaining few points tomorrow? Until then, many thanks to you and your skill and love for this world . . . good night my dear, mira

---

Journals and Correspondence

Subj: Re: Salaams for your Lovely Script
Date: 10/8/2002 11:38:39 AM E. Africa Standard Time
From: Julian Fellowes
To: Mira Nair

My dear

I am so pleased you are pleased. Nor do I disagree with a single one of your points so far. When in doubt let us always return to the book. As you will have seen I have put a lot of Thackeray back into it and, for me, the whole thing benefits from his presence.

Now, when do you need the fine-tuned version? I know you will say yesterday but I am actually in the middle of the house move which takes place next Tuesday. I will try my damnedest to get them done before then but this house is now like Borodino after the battle.

Once again, I am delighted. I can tell you now that I think it's one of the best things I've done and I know you're going to make a fabulous film.

Much love, Julian

From: Mira Nair
To: Julian Fellowes
Sent: Tuesday, October 08, 2002 6:28 PM
Subject: MN's remaining script notes

Dearest J,

As promised, here's what I left out last night:

7. A BIG NOTE: Let's omit Rawdon from performing the dance with Becky in front of Steyne. I think it castrates him completely and makes him appear ridiculous—which also puts Becky in a hugely unappealing light. I'm still dithering about what sort of dance this should be. . . but in any case, in terms of Rawdon, it should serve the purpose of him being increasingly sidelined in Becky's rise.

8. I remembered one line that Becky says to Rawdon from an earlier scene. I like the content of it, if only to remind the audience of the journey Becky has travelled alone: "One of us had to be bought. You let it be me."

9. The bigger, broader note I wanted to share with you is a cautionary one regarding the casting of the actors we wanted for 3 key roles: Dobb, Rawdon, and Lady Jane. One of the actors was concerned that in his memory from the TV series, Rawdon wasn't especially bright, a dullard, etc. I was, of course, giving him the line that it was in a way a genuine love story of two people who recognized each other well, and loved each other for it, and that he was a great father, blah, blah. Privately, I think it would be a great acting thing to behave in the bluff but tender way Rawdon has. . . . As for Dobbin, I still worry that he's a teeny-weeny bit one note: Mr. Unrequited Love. Have I misread it, you think? Anyway, in my notes I've tried to shave off some of his pathetic lines, but if there's any way he can be more "manly" (whatever!), it may help.

Drop the reference to the Governor's Mansion in Coventry Island. Too difficult. We should sell this scene for its hot, dusty, tropical world far from England. That's my final worry: whether we've made a hard enough sell for shooting these scenes in India. I wonder. As you know, Mr. Schamus prides himself for being cheap and I hope these won't be the first to go. Don't know if this is just a vague worry of mine though.

Becky enters Queen's Crawley to begin her employment as governess.

again, Julian, for letting
 ...eek of moving. But, what
 ...ting the noble battle with
 ...urse, they need to see the
 ...I mentioned to Glenn W.
 ...em by Friday, Oct. 11, so
 ...d. Was I bad to do so?
 ...ARLING.

 ...gy and more bite in this

 ...s

 ...rica Standard Time

My dear,

Thank you for these. Please do not curse me but I really do not think I can guarantee to have it with you by Friday. This is partly because the house is filled with men who are packing up the last twenty years of my life and asking for decisions every seven minutes, but it is also because there are some things that I simply must have a tiny bit of time to think about and get right.

Who has not seen how women bully women?

—William Makepeace Thackeray, *Vanity Fair*, 1847

Re your notes, I agree with pretty well everything. . . Of course the piano scene should feature the piano, I cannot think why I didn't do that. Though I appreciate all the notes about Miss Crawley, Jane, etc. enhancing the appeal of the parts, I am a little worried about the idea of fiddling with Rawdon to get an actor interested. I am happy to take him out of the charades but if Rawdon is not a bluff, unclever but attractive fellow then I believe the balance will go wrong. Becky's love for him (which I think we now have) is real but it is a protective love. If he is intelligent, then all his earlier pride in her will not work, nor will we feel sorry for him when the whole Steyne thing is going on. Indeed, we will think him in some way complicit. He will simply be another Dobbin character, but corrupted, and the whole lost-puppy element, which makes the stuff in the prison and the scenes with Jane so effective, will be missing.

But the only note I truly do not agree with is the one about Dobbin being too much a figure of "unrequited love." This, forgive me, smacks of the moment in a Hollywood script conference when one of the wet-eared executives says, "What is there in this movie for teenagers?" and gradually the precision of the narrative is dissolved into mush. The truth is, in the balance of this story, Dobbin does represent unrequited, or rather unappreciated, love. If you start to make him a dynamic suitor earlier in the story, then again his narrative will make no sense. Why would he trail after her for all those years if he is capable of taking control of his own love and giving it a proper value? My own belief is that the element that you sense missing from the character will be supplied not by new dialogue but by the actor's performance. If the actor is very firm and dynamic, then his choice not to corner Amelia and be demanding will be a strong choice.

Journals and Correspondence

I am only anxious, my darling Mira, not to deconstruct the balance of Thackeray's tale by trying to make every part fit the demands of particular players. Having said that, where this can be done without any damage to the piece as a whole then I am your man. (Incidentally, I do think that Lady Southwold and Mrs. Sedley have both now become worth playing and, at least for Lady S., it may be possible to get one of the famous dames of British Equity.)

Enough. Back to work and to my rather horrible life. Much love, Julian

---

From: Mira Nair
To: Julian Fellowes
Sent: Wednesday, October 09, 2002 10:48 PM
Subject: Lastly

darling J, I will now cook for you forever. U da best to do this so quickly, in the midst of the moving typhoon.

You're right to scold me about Dobbin. But I do hasten to tell you that the thought of American teenagers never once crossed my mind. . . I do confess, in all fairness, that it was a teeny-weeny worry of mine, and one that I only shared with you. Of course the scenes with him defending Amelia with Old Osborne et al will be dynamic and strong. So pardon moi.

What satisfying cinema this can be. I hope and intend to do it

In the novel, Thackeray describes Becky Sharp as being "tiny, red-headed and thin." When Mira Nair came upon this description, she took it as a sign that Reese Witherspoon was indeed the perfect Becky Sharp.

justice. Salaams, shukriya, thank you. Will raise the most exquisite claret in your name tonight (just as we prepare for war). You're heroic to even consider writing when your (not horrible) life is turned upside down. But I promise, in return, I'll come cook you a meal in your new mansion and we'll put away all the cutlery for it.

Much love, mn

Subj: Re: Lastly
Date: 10/13/2002 7:11:12 PM E. Africa Standard Time
From: Julian Fellowes
To: Mira Nair

This is the only message that could have lifted my spirits given that, thanks to the move, I am now in the third circle of Dante's Hell. I am really, really thrilled you like it. I truly think you are going to make the definitive version as well as a fantastic, remarkable film.

Much love as always, J.

MN: By the end of 2002, we had the shooting script, the locations in the city of Bath and Blenheim Palace, Churchill's home. With everything on schedule and my mind at once energized and at ease, I took off for a holiday down the Nile with my family with a plan to be back in London for the twelve weeks of pre-production in early January. Then the first crisis hit. The budget had to immediately be cut by one million dollars. Tax incentives dictated that we would now have to shoot the entire film in Ireland, but I tried to avoid being discouraged. It is the fate of a director to make every challenge an opportunity. I made a mad twenty-four-hour dash to Dublin with Declan Quinn, our veteran Irish cinematographer, to scout locations in our new country. Dublin was Georgian all right, but lacked the magnificence and grandeur of London. I wasn't thrilled with what I found, but our essential work would be to find solutions. We returned for a pow-wow in London to figure out the logistics of shipping in the sumptuousness, the hundreds of costumes, eighty horse-drawn carriages, equipment and props, so that we could keep to our start shooting date of March 15.

Then, as I finalised lists of Irish actors who could be cast as English with Mary Selway, our casting director, and slashed and burned the script with Julian to accommodate our newer, humbler locations in Ireland, one of our producers took me aside to say that our Becky Sharp, exhausted by the producing and starring demands of her most recent film, had called to say she wanted to postpone the shooting of the film to the fall.

With Reese's temporary withdrawal from the film, suddenly the problem wasn't the loss of Bath, but the loss of the entire film. When a film reaches the brink of production only to run into such a colossal impediment, there is the Humpty-Dumpty possibility of things falling apart never to be put together again. I left for Los Angeles to meet with Reese, suddenly fielding calls about two new projects I had earlier been interested in directing. No doubt everyone else in the film was looking at their own schedules. Reese sat with her feet up on my hotel couch, tiny and diminutive, yet so clear. I made my case for preserving the momentum and shooting in March, then listened to her describe her need for a longer break between the end of one film and the beginning of another. An actor's fragility is their power, I always say, so there was nothing for me to do but understand. We decided to resume prepping in May to film in August. I returned to my family in Kampala.

Journals and Correspondence

Suddenly, instead of making an epic film, I had to turn down the adrenaline and watch my garden grow.

In Kampala, I had something of a meltdown. It lasted two weeks. But as I drove my son to school, planted my mango trees, and caught up with my family over meals and homework, my equilibrium quietly returned. Then, one night, as I sat on our moonbench looking at the nightly carpet of stars, Reese was on the phone. She said, "Mira, I'm pregnant." I was delighted for her. And then she said, "Can we start filming tomorrow?" I was slightly dazed by this, yet elated. I called everybody, the good news being that we had to start right away but had to condense our 12 weeks of prep to 8 weeks, lest our star began to show. There wasn't enough time to fathom the logistics of filming in Ireland: the pregnancy gave me back England. Reese was so committed to playing Becky that she literally donated her entire salary to cover the additional costs of shooting in England.

From: Mira Nair
To: Julian Fellowes
Sent: Thursday, March 27, 2003 1:17 PM
Subject: hey darling one

hey julian—so sorry for the huge silence on my part for so long—what with the rollercoaster of VF, I was regaining my sanity planting mango trees in Kampala—and am now happy to be back in London going full-tilt towards production. Finally! Am back at the Knightsbridge, although have just found a lovely place in Fulham where I expect to move in a few days. How are you? I've heard lovely things about your script that you're about to direct—am sure you must be fully ensconced. Any chance of seeing you in London soonish??? I know you must be dreading doing more tinkering on VF, but as you well know

that is bound to happen. . . I have just a few things to talk to you about, and have pressed the studio to give me whatever notes they have so we can consolidate it all into one time.

Hoping you all are well (I have Peregrine jumping with the oscar on my fridge at home—too lovely) and inshallah I'll get to see you in your new mansion soon. . . much love, mn

---

Subj: Re: hey darling one
Date: 3/27/2003 6:56:33 PM Eastern Standard Time
From: Julian Fellowes
To: Mira Nair

My dear,

I have a big note on my desk: Write to Mira, so you have pipped me to the post.

I am SO delighted for you that the whole thing kicked in early. I know (no one better) what it is like trying to keep the flame alive as the months roll by. And I know you preferred the idea of filming in England so I am happy for that too.

Of course, I expected that there would be another round of tinkering on VF. Somehow I will fit it in so do not worry. My only concern at this late stage (because of previous experience) is not to let pointless notes from the studio take the edge off what is already a good script (always a danger). However, I am sure you and I are as one on this—as on everything—so I am relying on

Reese is an extraordinary listener. She was focused, brave, always open to trying things, and made it all seem incredibly effortless. —Mira Nair

Journals and Correspondence

you only to let the notes get through that YOU think are worth acting on. What you say needs looking at, I am delighted to look at.

I love you, Julian

P. S. The godson of a great friend of mine is trying to find one week of work experience on a film set in June. He is young, about seventeen, and as keen as mustard and all he wants to do is run errands and make tea and do what he's told for five working days near some REAL FILMING. He does NOT want to be paid so there is no question of finding any money. Would it be at all possible that he might come to help a bit on VF or does the thought fill you with horror? J.

Subj: Re: Notes
Date: 4/8/2003 4:15:50 AM Eastern Daylight Time
From: Julian Fellowes
To: Mira Nair

Dearest Mira,

I've received a message about holding off as the "production plan" is changing on *Vanity Fair*. What does that mean? Since most of your rewrites are to do with character delineation and emotional moments, I can't believe it will affect much of what we've talked about, will it? At any rate, I am still banging away at the notes from Friday's session but I thought I'd go through the other list one at a time as they are all quite contained. But first, I have used the "fluttering heart" line at Vauxhall. I put it into the carriage as they left the school but it seemed less effective than where it finally came to rest at the moment of expectation, when she is hovering with Amelia, trying to decide what the men are talking about just before the collapse of her hopes of Jos.

As for your notes, here goes:

1. Make clear George is Mr. Sedley's godson from the first Sedley scene. *Done. I have echoed this in the first Osborne dining scene.*

2. Jos should be included in the new Scene 10—in which Amelia plays the piano and Becky sings. He should be stuffing his face as he slowly falls in love with Becky and her singing—in parallel to Dobbin who enters and falls in love with Amelia as she plays the piano. *Done.*

3. I have always loved the image of Jos' hands bound in a web of the green silk with which Becky is making her purse. I know we've lost the whole purse idea, but is there any way at all you can think of including this image? It is so symbolic of the web Becky makes wherever she goes and could be splendidly cinematic. *Not done. My earlier e-mail explained why.*

4. And since we've made every single character come alive in this screenplay, can we add a line about Lady Crawley as well—perhaps in the montage VO—pg 162—(it is the essence of *Vanity Fair*) "her heart was dead long before her body. She had sold it to become Sir Pitt' Crawley's wife," and of course Thackeray goes on to say, "Mothers and daughters make the same bargain every day in *Vanity Fair*." Look it up in the book and perhaps you can make it clearer that it was a reference to the fact that she left her low-born love of her life to become a lady in suffering. *I tried this in the montage but it all seemed rather top-heavy so I have now put it into Miss Crawley's mouth at the news of her (Lady Crawley's) death. It fits, I think, with what we have just been saying, through Rawdon, about Miss C.'s snobbery when it comes to her own family.*

That's it. Much love, Julian

Subj: VF
Date: 4/13/2003 5:47:05 PM Eastern Daylight Time
From: Julian Fellowes
To: Mira Nair

My dear,

The pregnancy. Are you sure it will show? The great thing about the Regency fashions is that they could completely conceal the most advanced pregnancy and were used for just this purpose at the time. With no waist and stiff, rich materials falling from the bosom. . . ?

Having said that, I do not really know how to insert your pregnant love scene unless. . . How about the scene where Rawdon is getting ready to go to war after the ball? Suppose we have Becky already dressed for bed watching him strip off his uniform as he tells her about the money, the horse, etc. There is no longer any need for him to learn about the baby as he will have known it for ages.

My only sadness is that the whole point of Brussels, in Thackeray's concept, is that this is the one section of the story for Becky to show what she could achieve socially and in every other way if people would only let her. She is at the zenith of her beauty and of her power and Society there, unlike that of London later, opens up to receive her. Having her waddle through these scenes will, I am afraid, diminish the effectiveness of the Tufto plot and the sense that she is the sensation of Belgium will be gone. Are you absolutely positive that a good designer can't conceal it?

Subj: VF
Date: 4/13/2003 6:20:32 AM Eastern Daylight Time
From: Mira Nair
To: Julian Fellowes

Darlingest Julian

Yes indeed I did have to take off to LA where I am now. I have met Reese who looks divine, all glowing in her new condition.

MN: By now I had the great Hungarian costume designer Beatrix Pasztor (The Fisher King) *creating more than fifty looks for Becky, working carefully with corsets to camouflage "the bump." She skillfully layered feather and fur, paisleys and earthy indigos to make an enticingly hip Becky Sharp, looking closer to Gaultier than Laura Ashley. The benefits of Reese's pregnancy were manifold: her skin was luminous, her petite bosom now overflowed across Regency necklines, her fleshiness immensely appealing.*

Subj: VF
Date: 4/13/2003 6:20:32 AM Eastern Daylight Time
From: Julian Fellowes
To: Mira Nair

My dear,

I feel like a discarded lover sending a third (or is it a fourth?) e-mail with no answer from you. I have now implemented all the notes from our session plus the extra ones. I am rather pleased with the results and I long to give the script back to you. But there is talk of "production alterations" affecting the

Mira and I met a couple of years ago because I was a big fan of her work and was really excited to meet her. We have similar sensibilities about women, among other things. I thought she had an amazing take on *Vanity Fair* and the way she wanted to explore the roots of Indian culture in English society.

—Reese Witherspoon

The good news was that Thackeray had already given us about eighteen scenes in which Becky was pregnant. With Reese actually expecting, we increased that number to twenty-two scenes, scheduling them carefully toward the end of the shoot when she would be in full bloom. Reese's gift to me was giving me the idea of having a pregnant love scene on the night before Rawdon leaves for Waterloo. This was sweet reward for the endless challenges of camouflaging I had to employ: young children placed carefully in front of her in long lens to obscure Reese's bump; giving her large baskets or shawls to carry; or having carriages wipe across the screen at critical moments when Becky walks towards camera. The last thing I wanted to do was make a "talking heads" movie. We had to have a fluid, mobile camera, pregnancy or not, capturing a sense of freedom and the crackle of life. —Mira Nair

script... What can this mean? Do please reassure me that the studio is not now insisting that Becky marries Steyne and lives happily ever after.

Two whole locations are history with no real loss. In fact the Dobbin/George "She's dying" conversation coming just before George goes into meet Rhoda Swartz is an improvement and I do not miss the chapel at all. Becky's being pregnant (and its being known to all as it must be) slightly complicates George's offering to run away with her at the ball but since we absolutely must have this for the entire story to work, there is no point in getting into too much of a fix about it. I have given George a line to indicate that, pregnant or not, Becky is still much more attractive to him than his wife.

I hope they know they should thank you and your charms for achieving this. I suppose it is all part and parcel of the Hollywood thinking that the least important parts of a movie are the story and what the characters actually say to each other to tell it. . . Oh well, it was the same for Scott Fitzgerald and, thank God, you and I don't have to get involved.

I have incidentally repeatedly stressed to ICM that I have never had a single note from you that wasn't apposite, well judged and useful and that working with you has been an unmixed joy throughout. This I most truly feel.

Love, Julian

_____

From: Julian Fellowes
To: Mira Nair

You are going to make a terrific film. And I love you. The rest is mere detail. J.

_____

Journals and Correspondence

Subj: Your Notes
Date: 4/22/2003 6:30:21 AM Eastern Daylight Time
From: Julian Fellowes
To: Mira Nair

My dear,

With reference to your notes, my responses in italics:

13. SC 31. Is there any way you can include the charming and utterly modern nickname that was given to young Pitt at Eton—Miss Crawley? I thought it might be fun to have Rawdon tell Becky this as he's flirting with her about how bored she must be in QC. . . *Understood.*

14. SC 37. Add subliminal erotic fantasy—Rawdon kissing Becky. *Understood.*

15. SC 43. Complete re-write. Need a sexier, elegant scene, making clear that 1) Tilly would not approve of Becky for Rawdon and 2) Rawdon wants Becky but she won't let him touch her unless she's married. *Understood.*

16. Sc. 50. Becky tells Rawdon she's pregnant—now she's pregnant right through Brussels. *Understood.*

20. Sc 70. Add B & R making love at the end of this scene. *Understood.*

21. SC 80. Let Amelia have a flicker of doubt before she bids farewell to Dobbin. *Understood.*

22. SC 87. Add little Georgy pottering around, and to make Mrs. Sedley's litany about Dobbin be an ongoing theme from the middle of the film, roughly when Dobbin leaves A for India. *Understood.*

28. Make clear that George's and Amelia's match was made by the parents years ago. As in the book, Pg 143—George says, "haven't our papas settled it ever so long?" and "You and Sedley made the match a hundred years ago." *Understood.*

29. Change Ireland to seedy English sea-side resort. Make clear that Becky is not a whore. *Are you sure you don't want to go back to Germany? I cannot see that it requires much more than a title on the screen as almost the whole sequence is inside a gaming house, a hotel or a hotel courtyard. . . ? As for the whore bit, I had an idea of making Becky the dealer at a table. What do you think? It would show how far she has fallen without implications of prostitution.*

Subj: dire
Date: 4/29/2003 6:08:36 PM Eastern Daylight Time
From: Mira Nair
To: Julian Fellowes

my dear j, i'm afraid it looks dire. No more dough. We may have to lose the entire staging of the Vauxhall picnic. and we had another bloody blow today: we lost our one major location that was to house the slave dance, Becky's bedroom and George's wedding breakfast, thanks to your impoverished aristocracy insisting on a fee five times more than we can afford. i guess the themes of *Vanity Fair* are alive and kicking! i have felt defeated, but only because of the fever and flu. tomorrow we shall all rise again, inshallah. hope it's going well with you—ah the power of the pen—and hope to speak to you tomorrow.
love, mn

Subj: Re: dire
Date: 4/30/2003 4:40:11 AM Eastern Daylight Time
From: Julian Fellowes
To: Mira Nair

I am very sorry about your losing your first choice for the location, although the truth is there are other lovely houses and they will not require such a high fee to open their doors.

Love, J.

Subj: vanity fair—an appeal
Date: 5/7/2003 8:52:27 AM Eastern Daylight Time
From: Mira Nair
To: James Schamus

Dear James:

As we are almost upon the eve of commencing our shoot to make *Vanity Fair*, I feel I should let you know that I continue to feel throttled and compromised. In the true manner of one who has never had any excess money to make films, I have tried fullheartedly to cut, slash and burn this banquet of an epic to save every dollar we possibly can, to the point of an almost dangerous compression of the narrative. Already, we have cut the story to the point that so much of what is important in *Vanity Fair* happens off-screen (both Amelia and Becky's marriages, Waterloo, and of course, Vauxhall), any possible establishing shots/scenes of the different countries that we have in our story (Brussels, India, Germany)—all that is gone as well. In trying to get the contingency number to what you'd like it to be, I have demonstrated an alternative, in as passionate a way as I can, to Vauxhall (yet another key signpost associated with the novel along with Waterloo)—but I am writing you now that I cannot live with myself over this loss. In losing Vauxhall, we lose any political contextualisation of this time in England, we lose the explaining of the impact of the empire in creating the new middle-class that aspires to the status of the aristocracy—the milieu of our 5 main characters—and finally, we lose irony. We also, of course, lose any measure of my dis-

tinctive sensibility in bringing such a scene to life.

James, you know as well as I, that in many dramatic ways, this film resembles *Gone with the Wind*, and if allowed to be told right, could also share that film's popular appeal. In order to achieve that, it must have the cinematic sweep and magnificence, along with the humanist intimacy of the relationships that we have between our characters. We are at the risk of cutting most of that sweep out of the film. Please, James, don't hire me to make an epic and then force me to make a film that is now 90 percent (without exaggeration) shot in daytime interiors. Don't force the multilayered quality of this sprawling story into the chamber piece it is fast becoming. Don't hire a filmmaker who is known for visual flourish and excitement and have her make you a drawing-room drama. Your own press release announcing Focus' liaison with Mirabai Films prides me on being "a thoroughly contemporary filmmaker who excels at blending the traditional with the modern—which is precisely what a provocative new telling of *Vanity Fair* requires." Well, allow me to make that provocative new telling that you advertise.

What can I give up in return for the Vauxhall scene? I have scoured the script many times to provide an answer to this, but there is hardly any flab left. While I cannot bear to lose it completely, I would be willing to drastically reduce the opening of the movie to the extent that we can save a day of shooting. In the spirit of horse trading, I offer this day to you in exchange for Vauxhall and a masterful movie.

In addition, I have discussed with Julian about losing the three-page Orangery Scene celebrating Amelia's wedding to

FOLLOWING PAGES: Production designer Maria Djurkovic's sketch for the scene in Vauxhall Gardens.

Journals and Correspondence

George and cutting straight to Brussels—this we can do, but are loathe to do it, because it will be one of those dangerous compressions of time that I referred to earlier.

James, I guarantee you that made right, *Vanity Fair* will be one of your more memorable films as the head of the studio. At this final stage, with the hugely talented Reese Witherspoon with us as Becky Sharp, help us capture this encompassing vision and not reduce the uniqueness of our film into something perfectly viable but perfectly sedate. Remember it will be your film just as much as it will be mine. And as they say in India, your grandchildren will bless you for helping us!

with love and anticipation, mira

Subj: more notes from rehearsals etc
Date: 5/13/2003 9:45:15 AM Eastern Daylight Time
From: Mira Nair
To: Julian Fellowes

dearest julian, i was actually quivering with excitement last night as i read through the newest script. you are the fastest and the most eloquent (under pressure!). as i go through each day with the actors, i wanted to report some further little details that would be best be finessed by you. So here goes:

sc 10A: A tip from my friend Sooni: add the business here of Sedley doing accounts and getting more and more crumpled with worry before Mrs. S takes him to bed.

sc 31: Put in a bit of business here with Pitt giving Tilly some sort of pre-dinner delicacy which she promptly begins feeding to her lapdog. Becky sees this, and adds a line to her "I'm not sure I agree with you" line to Rawdon, saying something more about Tilly's humour and attitude....

Sc. 83: Add: "She's cut me out" to R's lines to make clear that he's been disinherited. James P. said this and it could actually sound quite poignant—although you could come up with something else if you think. . . ?? and also, should we have Becky make a reference to the fact that being a Crawley will enable them to live on nothing a year. . . hence Rawdon's reaction to her using the family name to forward themselves doesn't sit well. . .

all going strong—one love, mn

Subj: forgive me, another thing!
Date: 5/13/2003 10:01:44 AM Eastern Daylight Time
From: Mira Nair
To: Julian Fellowes

julian, sorry about this but i forgot to write a few more tidbits:

Sc. 57: I thought it could be interesting and lively if Dobs and George were horsing around fencing at home in the corridors (somewhat like the cricket we play in the corridors at home) instead of drinking sedately—then Old Os breaks it up, literally putting on a jacket over G's sweaty shirt as he leads him to meet Rhoda. Nice family dynamic.

Sc. 58: Do you think Rhoda could have a reference to her father's banana plantation fortune?

sorry Julian—I know you shall tire of me one day—but let that day not come soon! love, mn

---

Subj: Re: forgive me, another thing!
Date: 5/13/2003 11:07:51 AM Eastern Daylight Time
From: Mira Nair
To: Julian Fellowes

My dear,

I am sorry if, as I suspect, you want to lose the Cromwell line ("I'm her heir…"). This is partly because I love it but, more importantly, because it was one of my safeguards against the critics who are invariably determined to find that Hollywood has dumbed down yet another classic. Because the LA thinking is now commonly known, viz. that no line can ever be included which will not be understood by a food packer in Milwaukee, the critics are always keen to show that any American version of an English classic has combed out the book in question and served up a sub-intellectual treat. I just wanted one or two lines to show that this is absolutely not what we have been instructed to do. . .

MN: Keep it. No question. No dumbing down

On another note, I see major difficulties in the scene where you want the two Osborne men fencing. It is totally unrealistic that these two young men would be fencing or wrestling in a dining room and since we are only allowed two interiors in the Osborne house (and Rhoda is quite properly in the other one) I don't know how to solve this. I am stumped. Can they mock up a bedroom for George where they could do what they liked?

MN: Sadly not. OK, OK, OK, maybe i got carried away with my actors—but still can't they be doing something physical instead of just talking over port? I was inspired by the memory of my brothers perpetually playing cricket in our corridors. . .

Second, I am unwilling to put in a reference to bananas for the black heiress from Jamaica. We are already wonderfully close to the wind and are only protected by the fact that you are the most politically correct person known to man. Would you be happy with a sugar plantation (much more likely in Jamaica anyway)?

MN: Why darling, are you suggesting that it would be racist to suggest bananas? Ok, sugar is better. . .

Otherwise, I shall get on with the rest of them. When do you need them?

MN: Why don't i finish my rehearsals with steyne/becky on friday, email you any further notes, and you do it all at once by the weekend?? Rehearsals going well.

Love, MN

From: Mira Nair
To: Julian Fellowes.
Sent: Monday, July 28, 2003 11:29 PM
Subject: Re: Dialogue

darling j, thanks for your understanding but please understand that i will honour your music to its utmost—and to that effect have always consulted you on every syllable that i can. the jos sedley scene went fantastically and will be entirely possible for me to cut it to its bare bones. lydia had a valuable idea yesterday when she saw the 2 hr 45 minute cut of the movie. she suggested a scene of Sir Pitt dying, especially as in Hoskins' hands he is such a lovable character. His dying off screen is too perfunctorily presented. So how about a scene inspired by the book, him on his deathbed tended by Horrocks, giving him a monologue (short) about whom he should leave his money to? It could be funny and rueful. Do think about it and let me know. Counting the last days, yours truly mn

---

Subj: Re: Dialogue
Date: 7/29/2003 11:37:37 AM GMT Daylight Time
From: Julian Fellowes
To: Mira Nair

I love this idea. Too many people die and marry off screen and to wind up as powerful a performance as Bob's properly and well seems absolutely right. I attach my first go at it. Of course

it also explains R's & B's predicament for the next sequence so much more clearly.

Love, Julian

After wrapping up the shoot in London, I returned to New York to spend weeks in the editing room. On the seventh of November, we finally revealed the director's cut—a 2 hour, 45 minute version of the film—to James Schamus, the co-head of Focus Features, and his team of production executives. At the end of the film, James looked at me and said, "I'm dazzled... This is a big movie, an emotional movie." (The wife of the COO came up to me later and said that in all her husband's years of seeing rough cuts, she had never seen him have such a passionate response.) I had a honeymoon for like a week and then, of course, the notes started coming. For that one week though, I felt like a goddess.

Yet despite their enthusiasm, I was unhappy with the ending. A humbled and widowed Becky returns to Sir Pitt's house to see her son. Young Rawdy is being raised by Rawdon's brother, who inherited the wealth that had been meant for Rawdon before his inopportune marriage to Becky. One wintry day in January, while lunching with my agent, Bart Walker, I sud-denly found myself describing an ending that I thought would work. This denouement picked up on my earlier insistence that in order to be classed as a true epic, rather than a costume drawing-room drama, Vanity Fair needed scenes from another world. With Bart's encouragement, I scheduled another meeting with Focus and painted the picture of a finale in India. In this, I took Thackeray's heroine back to the land in which he was born.

We had created two Indian scenes in England, the Colchester Sand Quarry for Rajasthan and the stately marble interior of Elveden for the wrestling rooms of Bikaner, so going to India to film meant that we could finally augment these scenes with glorious landscapes. I also could finally shoot one of my favourite scenes we had earlier lost—Rawdon savagely tying Becky's corsets as their marriage begins to crumble. I didn't want to trouble the baby, but now Deacon Reese Phillippe was here, and his mother had returned to her tiny waist. So we booked The Windsor Room in the Umaid Bhavan, the statuesque Art Deco palace built by the Maharaja of Jodhpur in the middle of the desert, re-created Mayfair, and filmed England in India.

The Empire had managed to do this trick on a grand scale. Now it was the return of the native.

George Osborne (Jonathan Rhys Meyers) and Rhoda Swartz (Kathryn Drysdale) are introduced by George's father who wants them to marry. "In a perverse way," says Nair, "I wanted Rhoda to be the most beautiful woman in the film. The dress she wore in this scene was the fifth costume designed for her and the one which I finally approved."

William Makepeace Thackeray: The History of *Vanity Fair*

William Makepeace Thackeray, the only child of Richmond and Anne Becker Thackeray, was born on July 18, 1811 in Calcutta. His father worked in the service of the East India Company and died when William was five years old. The following year the boy was sent to England to be educated, as was the fashion for colonial-born children. Shortly after William departed India by himself, his mother remarried her first love, Captain Henry Carmichael-Smyth, and they joined William in England three years later.

Unhappy at school, William became an avid reader and sketch artist. He entered Trinity College at Cambridge in 1829 (where he lost a poetry contest to Alfred Tennyson) but left before obtaining his degree. He studied law but supported himself by selling sketches and working in an office. He loved to gamble, incurred some major debts, and ran through a small inheritance received in 1832. He returned to Paris in 1834 to study art and, two years later, married Isabelle Shaw. Their first child, Anne Isabella, was born in 1837. To support his family, Thackeray began writing magazine articles and sold two popular series to two different publications. Though his writing career began to flourish, his personal life floundered. A second daughter died at less than a year old. Though a third daughter, Harriet Marian, was born in 1840 and thrived; his wife did not. She fell victim to some kind of mental illness, became suicidal, and was placed in a private institution where she remained for the rest of her life. (Isabelle would outlive her husband by thirty years and be a great burden to her daughters.)

Throughout the next decade, Thackeray published several books including *The History of Henry Esmond*, *The Newcombes*, and *The Book of Snobs*. In 1848, *Vanity Fair* was published in eighteen monthly installments, establishing him as a one of the most popular novelists of his day. Influenced by Henry Fielding, Thackeray had the ability to re-create society in satirical portraits of enduring vitality. He was popular on the lecture circuit and made two visits to America, in 1852 and 1855, delivering popular speeches which were published in *The English Humorists of the 18th Century*.

RIGHT: Portrait of William Makepeace Thackeray, January 1, 1860.

His health was always precarious. He suffered from recurring kidney infections caused by a bout of syphilis in his youth. Still, he managed to build an impressive estate and settle generous dowries on his two daughters. His youngest, known as Minnie, married Leslie Stephen, had one daughter, and died suddenly at the age of thirty-five. (Leslie later remarried and had another daughter, Virginia Woolf, the famous writer).

In 1863, Thackeray realized that he was seriously ill, and he visited his old friends to say farewell. He died on Christmas Eve, 1864, at the age of fifty-three, while working on a novel called *Denis Duval*. Over 2,000 mourners attended his funeral, including Charles Dickens.

Of Thackeray's gifts, the imminent literary critic V. S. Pritchett has observed, "Thackeray was the first of our novelists to catch visually and actually life as it passes in fragments before us, a gift that brings him close to modern novelists as different as Proust and the cinematic reporters—a Hemingway, say, or a Graham Greene. He certainly invented the modern non-hero."

Thackeray's drawing, RIGHT, of Sir Pitt Crawley proposing to Becky Sharp from the original publication of *Vanity Fair*, and the same scene as depicted in the movie, LEFT.

Creating the Map of Life: Casting *Vanity Fair*

The map of life of any film is in the faces of those whom we choose, and Mary Selway knew that better than any of us. Between Nair's long tradition of "intuitive casting" where she mixed non-actors with movie stars (Denzel Washington opposite Sarita Choudhury in Mississippi Masala, *Naseeruddin Shah opposite members of her own family in* Monsoon Wedding*), and Mary's long and distinguished career, the casting of* Vanity Fair *was a huge and colorful task. It took almost eight months and involved meeting more than 500 actors in England and America to finally arrive at our own map of life of Thackeray's sparkling ensemble of characters.*

REESE WITHERSPOON

From the beginning, there was no Becky Sharp for me other than Reese. I'd marveled at her work in *Election* and had never forgotten the stillness of her gaze in *The Man in the Moon*. Precisely because I wanted to retain the complicatedness of Becky's character, I wanted an actor who could be all that whilst being utterly irresistible to watch. Reese does precisely that: she is beguiling, comic, steelily intelligent, and radiant at the same time. The world had seen her do her adorable comic turn before—but in

Vanity Fair, my inspiration was to have her emerge into a full-blown sensual woman.

RHYS IFANS

Dobbin's character was familiar to me from scores of Hindi movies—the hero's best friend afflicted by unrequited love—usually played by the "silent-yet-deadly" actors like Raaj Kumar or Rajendra Kumar. Dobbin was the moral center of the story, and needed to be played by an actor who was not afraid of being transparent about his love, yet not be boring in suffering. I had met all of England's up-and-coming and up-and-arrived for this role, wanting the choice to have the energy of surprise. Then Mary thought of Rhys Ifans, and sent me to see his brilliant performance in *Accidental Death of an Anarchist* at the Donmar. Like everyone in the world, I thought him

A portrait of the faces in *Vanity Fair* from the scene celebrating the marriage of George and Amelia: Standing (from left): Joseph Sedley (Tony Maudsley); George Osborne (Jonathan Rhys Meyers); George Dobbin (Rhys Ifans). Seated: Rawdon Crawley (James Purefoy); Becky Sharp (Reese Witherspoon); Amelia Sedley (Romola Garai).

Casting Vanity Fair

Becky Sharp
REESE WITHERSPOON

Rawdon Crawley
JAMES PUREFOY

William Dobbin
RHYS IFANS

George Osborne
JONATHAN RHYS MEYERS

Amelia Sedley
ROMOLA GARAI

one of the great physical comic actors, like Tati. But then, having spent an evening with him and his girlfriend Jessica at the BAFTAs last year, I remembered how his face had just suffused with love at the sight of her. There I saw the poet in him beyond the clown. In his gangly form, Rhys provides the shorthand we need to indicate immediately why he would be overlooked by Amelia, but then—with his greatness as an actor, his beautiful voice, his face in repose, his soulfulness and surrender to the thankless love he feels—I guarantee you he will steal our hearts. Much like the performance of Vijay Raaz, the tent man in *Monsoon Wedding*, who at first seems coarse and vulgar and then, with his vulnerability at being undone in love, becomes unforgettable—that is indeed Dobbin's trajectory in *Vanity Fair*, and one that Rhys Ifans delivers with aching splendor, lightness, and poignancy.

JAMES PUREFOY

It took us a long time to find Rawdon. James was playing the dragon in a big kid's movie in the snow, and Mary sent him to see me in New York. He came into my office and all the girls swooned. I asked my assistant to read opposite him and in the scene, he had to kiss her. She was just sweating. Purefoy is Rawdon in life. A New Age James Bond, I would jokingly call him. Dashing, brave, he is the kindest father to his own son Jojo, who is so much like Rawdy. Mary knew he could be heartbreaking. I also really liked the idea of not pairing a movie star against another movie star, because when you do that, it becomes a movie stars' movie. I liked the idea of a somebody fairly unknown and fresh, stealing upon us from sideways, unexpectedly.

JONATHAN RHYS MEYERS

Like Marilyn Monroe is shorthand for sex, George Osborne had to be shorthand for vanity, arrogance, and dangerous beauty—and the only person in my mind was Johnny Rhys Meyers. I knew the role was for him before we even began to cast. He is pure eye candy, but with soul and mischief. The beauty of JRM is that he's just a little boy underneath all that gorgeousness. . . .

| Joseph Sedley
TONY MAUDSLEY | The Marquess of Steyne
GABRIEL BYRNE | Miss Matilda Crawley
EILEEN ATKINS | Sir Pitt Crawley
BOB HOSKINS | Pitt Crawley
DOUGLAS HODGE |

ROMOLA GARAI

Amelia was a cinch from the beginning. I saw a host of great actresses on either side of the Atlantic, but had seen Romola in "Daniel Deronda" on television in my hotel room one night and was hooked. It was a done deal. I literally cast her without meeting her—she was filming abroad at the time, we chatted on the phone and I met her months later on our set. What a gem, our Romola. Fire and unbridled truth in her, such a far cry from the simpering Amelia that she could so easily have become.

EILEEN ATKINS

Mary sent me to see Eileen A. in the play *Honor* and she was riveting. Not an untruthful bone in her body. I loved her gravelly voice and handsome demeanor. And the map of life on her face—she was fairly instantly Tilly. I had based some of Tilly's character on a friend of mine in Bombay, a wealthy heiress who once said that it is the privilege of the rich to be as uncouth as possible. Eileen loved being asked to "let it rip" and she went for it, full-tilt.

Like many rich, single women, we thought Aunt Tilly could be constantly pampered onscreen—baths, manicures, pedicures, you name it. These are things we never see in films from the period, and Eileen just loved doing all that. The day before we were to do the scene in the bath, she came up to me and said, "I'd like to offer you my arse." I had wanted her to leap out of the bath like a young girl, but when she made that memorable offering, I found myself taking a pair of scissors and cutting the canvas apron off her! She loved it, standing there naked as a child. . . it gets the biggest roar of laughter, Eileen's arse.

GABRIEL BYRNE

Who doesn't like to look at Gabriel? I'd carried a torch for him for many years, and find him compelling and mysterious. He specifically brought something to the role which perhaps Thackeray did not intend but which I love: the quest for soul. We reinvented Steyne as a ruthless man who loved art. It's very easy to play the superficial,

Casting Vanity Fair

Lady Jane Sheepshanks
NATASHA LITTLE

Mr. Osborne
JIM BROADBENT

Lady Southdown
GERALDINE MCKEWAN

Mrs Sedley
DEBORAH FINDLAY

Lady Steyne
KELLY HUNTER

unfeeling aristocrat, but it's much more difficult and interesting to play somebody who has everything except that which he needs: the desire to be loved and to love. Gabriel surrendered completely to that slack-jawed way of speaking that the English aristocracy have, creating a Steyne who was at once ruthless, poignant, and sexy.

JIM BROADBENT

To be able to work with the legendary Jim Broadbent, I would die happier. I was so honored when he said yes immediately. He has no vanity at all in his work; his acting has such humility, huge range, and complete versatility. There's no one way to approach any character, each one is multifaceted, and with Old Osborne, I wanted Jim to play him as a person who is not only a curmudgeon obsessed with status and pretension, but also as a father besotted with the beauty and spirit of his son, George. Jim played all shades of Osborne in such a deeply human manner—working with him is like fine-tuning an extraordinary instrument.

GERALDINE MCKEWAN

Was another Mary idea. I wanted someone very different from Aunt Tilly and with comic potential. I'd learned from *Monsoon Wedding*, also a film with 68 actors, how each one had to be cast as distinctive from the other. I'd seen Geraldine in *The Magdalene Sisters*, where she played the nastiest nun in the world. When we met, I loved her birdlike face (which is what inspired those Tweety-bird sounds she makes as Lady Southdown), her tiny-tiny eyes, she's another map of life. The years of experience that an English actor carries from stage to screen and back was so huge in terms of Eileen and Geraldine; they were fantastic together in the comic scenes and gave of themselves completely.

NATASHA LITTLE

Played Becky Sharp in the BBC mini-series of *Vanity Fair*, and the minute I met her in my hotel room, I was struck by the almost spiritual honesty and purity in her—just the quality for Lady Jane. I told Mary I would not make the film without her. Natasha just glows, and perhaps because she got married while we were shooting, she was all the more luminous. She brought her wedding cake to the set the day we shot the slave dance, and I bit straight into the sixpence she had hidden in the cake. I didn't know it was English tradition for the best good luck—Natasha almost wept with happiness when I handed her the coin!

DOUGLAS HODGE

We must have met scores of actors for Pitt, but I fell in love with Douglas very quickly because of his blithe quality and most exquisite sense of comedy. He would make us cry with laughter during the dinner-table scenes. Pitt could so easily have been merely pompous and insufferable, but in Douglas' hands, he was played with lightness and wit. I thought he and Purefoy made excellent brothers as well, serving as the perfect foils to each other.

BOB HOSKINS

The beauty of making a film with such a large ensemble cast is that one can approach so many actors that one deeply admires. *Mona Lisa* is one of my all-time favorite films, and it was such a complete pleasure to have Bob Hoskins in our film. Once again, we wanted a surprising choice for Pitt Crawley, and nobody asks Bob to be in period films. Both Mary and I knew he would be the perfect unpretentious country squire with a naughty twinkle in his eye, and not take himself seriously at all. He's just

the sort of actor who picks everybody up with his energy and humor, and of course lights up the screen as a result.

ALL THE OTHERS

For Mr. Sedley, John Franklyn-Robbins came in and made us all cry. Deborah Findlay, as Mrs. Sedley, was extraordinary in her range, as was the unforgettable Kelly Hunter, who played Lady Steyne with such brittle perfection. Lucy Bevan, Mary's trusted assistant, brought us the most amazing children to see for the parts of Young Becky, Rawdy, and Georgy. Tom Sturridge as Young Georgy had the exact uncanny beauty as Jonathan Rhys Meyers (his father in the story). In the one quick scene he had, I wanted him to be shorthand for that same blazing beauty and petulance that his father possessed.

Often actors came in to read for one role, and would be offered another. That's what happened with Richard McCabe, the great stage actor, who came in to read for Pitt and ended up getting cast as the King. Or Jonny Phillips, who read for Dobbin and became Wenham. It was a surfeit of riches, and if the actors were game, why not have them all in the film? The same happened with Sophie Hunter who played Maria Osborne—I knew Thackeray had written her as an old maid, but I went weak in the knees at Sophie's beauty and skill.

My feeling is that if we ask people to pay ten bucks to watch our film, let's give them a treat when they enter our world.

—Mira Nair

46

Layering the Façade: Costumes and Hairstyles

Beatrix Pasztor might seem, to some, an unlikely costume designer to hire for *Vanity Fair*. There are many designers who have won Oscars for period costumes but, previously to working on this film, Pasztor had only designed contemporary costumes. Yet Mira had loved Pasztor's work ever since she saw Terry Gilliam's *Fisher King* and Gus Van Sant's *Even Cowgirls Get the Blues*.

"I wanted *Vanity Fair* to be as far from a 'frock movie' as possible," explains Nair. "I interviewed all the usual suspects but it was Beatrix who captured my imagination with her untraditional designs. Everything is up for use in her eyes: feathers, frayed fabric, rope." Such work fit into Nair's vision that "this film was about layers and sham and façade; about seeing what was underneath things."

Pasztor and Nair both came at the material in the same way. They did not want the movie to look like any other film. To this end, they reviewed other films and said to each other, "This is what we don't want it to be."

What they wanted was inspiration from the period and, for that, Pasztor turned to the novel. "Thackeray described costumes very well in the book and I tried to use some of his details and build costumes from his guidelines while introducing new textures," says the designer. "The silhouettes and shapes were of the era and we used wonderful ruffled seams that were all hand-made as there would not have been easy access to sewing machines at that time. With hand stitching and gathering on pieces of fabric we created beautiful decorations on the costumes."

Pasztor also made the actor's costumes a little tighter than usual. "I like small clothes on people because I think it gives them character," she says. "So, all the actors were wearing a little bit tighter clothes than they should because this changes the proportion and the look."

As for the color palette, Pasztor took inspiration from India. "The influence of India is evident throughout the

George Osborne (Jonathan Rhys Meyers), William Dobbin (Rhys Ifans), and Rawdon Crawley (James Purefoy) in their magnificent military dress uniforms, worn for the ballroom scene.

Costumes and Hairstyles

RIGHT: *Odalisque: Woman of Algiers*, by Pierre-Auguste Renoir, 1870, was only one of many paintings that inspired the costumes in *Vanity Fair*. BELOW: Original costume drawings for the movie by Beatrix Pasztor.

film with the use of different fabrics and textures," she explains. "We used these very strong Indian colors all the way through including purples, oranges, and patterns, while also mixing in the muted English style. I took certain liberties with the decoration; it was a free-flying process. We lost all the rigidity from the period."

Layering was a crucial element to all of the costumes in keeping with Nair's concept that everything in *Vanity Fair* was covered up or hidden behind layers of façade. "When actors came for fittings we would put one cravat, one waistcoat, and one coat on them, and they would think that this was the end of the fitting," explains Pasztor. "However I started layering the costumes and creating an excess which made the costumes richer."

Actor Bob Hoskins was astounded by the amount of layering that went into his costume. "I think Beatrix was paid by how many clothes she could put on you!" jokes the actor. "I had about fifteen waistcoats on and she tried to put these neckties on me; there were more and more going on and I suddenly had no neck left. It was incredible and it definitely created a different look—I felt like a highwayman sinking inside this closet!"

Nair adds that there "was a lovely new slang expression on the set because of Beatrix's layers. When the actors came out of

wardrobe, we would say they had been 'Beatrixed,' meaning they were swathed in layers."

The experience was new to actor Gabriel Byrne. "It's the only film I've ever worked on where the grips said, 'Those costumes are nice, aren't they?' When the costumes get noticed by the guys who are humping around lights and pieces of wood, that's pretty rare. On the other hand I've seen movies where the costumes swamp the story and it becomes a moving costume spectacle." That was not the case on *Vanity Fair*. "Beatrix dresses each character as opposed to each actor," explains Byrne. "Even the materials on the extras costumes were absolutely ingenious and original."

There were more than sixty-seven speaking roles in *Vanity Fair* which meant hundreds of costumes were needed. And considering that each outfit involved many layers, the sheer volume of clothing was staggering. Pasztor partly solved this problem by rotating pieces of clothing. "Secretly I was reusing, or recycling, pieces of clothing, especially the pieces that were worn underneath because they were not seen," she says. "It was hard to find good pieces. I could

RIGHT: Bob Hoskins, who plays Sir Pitt Crawley, joked that since he had to wear so many layers of clothing, he assumed that costume designer Beatrix Pasztor was "paid by how many clothes she could put on you!" LEFT: Jonathan Rhys Meyers and Tony Maudsley in the Vauxhall scene.

Costumes and Hairstyles

not make pieces for everyone and the costume houses in England were very limited. Our saving grace was a costume house in Paris that had incredible pieces for us to use. Mira loves fashion and was always encouraging me to go more towards Vivienne Westwood and Jean Paul Gaultier than the more traditional. The fun was in the layering and invention."

Mira's goal for the costume designs was simple. "I want everyone to want these clothes," she told Beatrix.

Though everyone joked about the layering and the amount of clothing each actor wore, at the end of the day, this attention to detail proved beneficial. "I think most of the actors enjoyed the process," says Pasztor, "as it helped them to define their character." This was certainly true for Rhys Ifans who plays Dobbin. "This was my first period film," he says, "and I've never been so informed by a costume, it makes you stand differently and speak differently."

Like the costume designs, the hairstyles in *Vanity Fair* combined aspects of traditional period styles with Indian influences and a modern sensibility. Jenny Shircore, hair and makeup artist, was responsible for using diverse elements to create hairstyles that wouldn't overwhelm the actors.

"Mira's enthusiasm encouraged me to take this film," explains Shircore, who has won an Academy Award for her

Costumes and Hairstyles

work on Shekhar Kapur's *Elizabeth*. "The bigger, bolder, brighter aspect of the work come from Mira. As in her other films, Mira pushes things in that direction. But we can't ever lose sight of where we're coming from, and the rules that are established by the period of the work. We've stretched the period, though, played with it and enjoyed it."

The rules were indeed stretched to the limit in the extravagant, often towering, hairstyles created for Reese Witherspoon. Shircore began with period designs such as Apollo knots, which are large pieces of hair shaped into bows; then she added fanciful details with feathers, ribbons, and bits of jewelry. "The period sits quite comfortably on Reese," says Shircore. "If an actress doesn't wear it well, you can't use it. But Reese could carry it off easily."

Many wigs were used and, at the insistence of Mira Nair, the actors often removed them on screen. Nair wanted to make a point of what it was really like to dress in those days and the amount of work that went into creating the fashion. In one scene, Eileen Atkins (Matilda Crawley)

ABOVE: Jenny Shircore, hair and makeup artist, on set during production. RIGHT (clockwise from top left): Joseph Sedley (Tony Maudsley), Matilda Crawley (Eileen Atkins), William Dobbin (Rhys Ifans), and Becky Sharp (Reese Witherspoon) showing the range and variety of hairstyles designed by Shircore.

Jenny never stopped. Like Becky Sharp, she paid equal attention to the courtier and the king. No actor, whether an extra or movie star, escaped the sheer joy of her skill. —Mira Nair

pulls her wig off and scratches her head, letting the audience know how uncomfortable it was to be wearing it. Other scenes showing Atkins bathing and being manicured stressed the point that getting dressed and groomed in those days involved a great deal of work and the help of many servants. "Usually movies only show pretty montages of beautiful people in beautiful settings," says Nair, "but I wanted the audience to see the reality behind this process. It was one way to make the people and the story timeless and not removed from today's reality."

Indeed, the sculpted hairstyles created by Shircore involved a team of stylists and hundreds of hours of preparation. One can only imagine how much more difficult the process was two hundred years ago.

From Bath to Jodhpur: Locations

The best compliment I heard while filming was when Barry Brown (editor, *Salaam Bombay!*) visited the Bath set. He looked at the four boulevards we had shut down and smothered with peat, horses, carriages, button vendors, apple sellers, and hundreds of people and said, "This feels like *Salaam Bombay!*" He got it. We were going for the filth, the coal-shoveling and the pigs, laced around the edges of our story, just to make clear that life was proliferating in all directions, to show how much the working classes had to do to allow the upper classes to live like they did. . . It was *that* approach rather than making anything too pretty. We went for the jugular on color, on the clothing, and the sets. —Mira Nair

The exterior shots for the London scenes were filmed in Bath, which has some of the best-preserved Regency architecture in the country. A massive effort was mounted to get permission to close off the streets for four days of shooting.

*I*t was always the intention of director Mira Nair to film a portion of *Vanity Fair* in her native India. She wanted to avoid making her movie look like an English drawing-room piece and to capture the hot light of India, a country whose wealth and refinement had greatly influenced the aesthetic of Thackeray's novel.

Colonial influences of the era were a great inspiration to production designer Maria Djurkovic. "The whole film is set in the first quarter of the nineteenth century, a time when Britain had colonies all over the world," explains Djurkovic. "I suppose one of the key elements to the look of Regency England was references that came from the colonies—the Indian, the North African and even the Chinese influences. I surrounded myself with these references that reflect the colors and the vibrancy of all those influences. This was something that we felt was very important to convey in the film."

But, since the novel actually takes place in England, most of it was filmed in locations around southern England during the spring of 2003. The scenes for Queen's Crawley were filmed at Stanway House, near

Locations

Cheltenham. The home of Sir Pitt Crawley needed to be extravagant but, at the same time, appear somewhat run-down and neglected and Stanway House was the perfect embodiment of this concept. "Stanway House was the first location I saw for the film," says Mira Nair. "Declan [Quinn, the director of photography] and I fell in love with it instantly, and actually designed scenes and had scenes re-written to reflect the location. I loved the Indian ochre-colored stone with its feeling of lived-in decay, the George Romney paintings, and the heirloom chinoiserie beds that were completely part and parcel of my own sensibility about making *Vanity Fair* come alive."

After her short stay as governess in Queen's Crawley, Becky travels to London with Matilda Crawley and her nephew, Rawdon Crawley. The exterior shots for these scenes were filmed in Bath, which has some of the best-preserved Regency architecture in the country. "We were very lucky with Bath because we had a very large street which was in almost pristine condition, and once some gravel and dirt had been put on the road we were suddenly in the 1800s," says Quinn. "It meant we could cre-

LEFT: *The Green Cabinet* from W. H. Pynes' *Royal Residences*, 1819. This is an example of Chinoiserie design that was used as inspiration for the Queen's Crawley interiors. RIGHT: Production designer Maria Djurkovic's illustration of the living room at Queen's Crawley; a photograph of the finished set appears on page 60-61.

ate big, rich, busy vistas without the worry of modern buildings getting in the way."

Naturally, a great deal of work went into creating the look of the era. "We accomplished hugely ambitious stuff in Bath, shooting right down Great Pulteney Street and see-ing three hundred and sixty degrees," explains Maria Djurkovic. "Doing that in any modern town is a big number and involves closing roads and covering road surfaces, taking away road signs and painting windows and doors and bringing in all the horses and carriages and so on. Mira was very keen on animals providing life on the street. We brought in truckloads of pigs for the first scene, a herd of cows for Bath, mangy dogs for the carnage at Waterloo,

and goats and sheep for the escape from Brussels."

Creating the scope and grandeur of these exteriors was crucial to the scene where Becky first arrives on Curzon Street. "Her carriage heads towards the largest mansion on the street," explains producer Janette Day. "Much to Becky's frustration, they drive on past and stop at one of the Georgian terraces. She can see the mansion from her window and it tantalizes her—this is where she wants to be. I think it's worth the enormous work we've had to put into setting up the scenes here in order to establish that wonderful geography at the heart of the film."

The interior scenes of the Curzon Street house were shot

Locations

at Fitzroy Square in Central London. Also in Bath, the Holburne Museum was transformed into Steyne's mansion, and Beaufort Square became the Osborne residence. That transformation included the addition of many colonial influences. "We made a very deliberate choice to go for a really quite strong palette of colors," says Djurkovic, "to use a lot of oriental influences, whether it's in textiles or papers, or even in the choice of locations themselves. It's a mixture of everything—Chinese gongs, Moroccan lanterns, and Indian 'mushroo' fabrics that we had shipped from India."

The movie filmed at a number of other stately homes in England, including Ditchley Park in Oxfordshire (the interior of the Crawley house), Wrotham Park in Hertfordshire (the interior of the Gaunt House), West Wycombe Park in Buckinghamshire (the interior of the Sedley House), and Luton Hoo in Bedfordshire, where several interiors were filmed.

The production also had the opportunity to work in Hampton Court Palace, which represented Hyde Park and some of the exteriors of Brussels. The Brussels

On the first day of location scouting, a year before shooting began, Nair and Quinn fell in love with Stanway House. The fantastic chinoiserie beds with the elaborate canopies delighted the filmmakers and were included in the shot.

countryside and the aftermath of the Battle of Waterloo were shot at Hatfield House.

In the end, the filmmakers had less than a week of shooting in India. The last scene featuring Becky Sharp and Jos Sedley atop an elephant was shot over a period of four days on location at the Mehrangarh Fort. Located on the hilltop that rises sharply at the city of Jodhpur in northwest India, Mehrangarh (which means "majestic fort") was founded in 1459 and encloses many palaces.

By shooting in India and incorporating colonial influences in the production design, the filmmakers were able to expand the look of *Vanity Fair* and capture the essence of Regency England. Unlike many other movies set in this period, *Vanity Fair* takes us out of the drawing room and into Thackeray's tumultuous world of high and low society.

LEFT: Angelica Mandy as the young Becky Sharp in one of the opening scenes from the film. ABOVE: *Kutpootlee Nautch, Alias Fantoccini* (On My Veranda), by William Prinsep, c. 1827, was another inspiration for the filmmakers. BELOW: Production designer Maria Djurkovic.

The Look of the Film: Production Design

*D*irector of Photography, Declan Quinn, has worked with Mira Nair on four of her previous films: Monsoon Wedding, Hysterical Blindness, 9.11.01, and Kama Sutra. *Long before they began shooting, Quinn and Nair had many discussions about the look of the film and how they would approach filming it. The following discussion recounts many of the ideas they initially discussed, along with the movies that served as inspiration and the challenges they faced during the production.*

OVERALL LOOK & STRATEGY

MIRA NAIR: It was true what you said yesterday that we actually didn't start out thinking what this film should look like but more what it should not look like. I wanted to be as far as possible from a period frock movie, or anything approaching the dull competence of *Masterpiece Theatre* or a stodgy drawing room drama.

DECLAN QUINN: *The Duellists* was definitely a big influence, but when it came down to shooting *Vanity Fair*, the kind of contrast in that film didn't work in ours. In *The Duellists*, there are mostly two characters in big rooms or big landscapes, so they could get very gutsy with the light. In *Vanity Fair*, there are rooms full of characters who need enough light to be seen when they're speaking.

NAIR: More than the light, *The Duellists* taught me how to not make a set feel precious. Scott treated a ballroom like he would a stable. What I wanted to do was to get beyond the grandeur of what we were seeing to the core of it, the sham of it, the bad wigs, or whatever else made life tick. I wanted to make it feel like we were present at every moment, in every frame.

QUINN: *The Duellists* was very good that way. The handheld camera didn't make anything precious. It had the democratic treatment of situation.

NAIR: And you felt the frayed collars, and the kind of raggedy, long hair that was unwashed, as they dueled. It felt extremely real. You felt the perspiration, you felt that they didn't change their clothes very often, things like that, and also I reveled in the peculiarity of the casting. I was happily surprised to discover that we shared the same casting director, the inimitable Mary Selway. Remember how peculiar Keith Carradine looked? And how Harvey Keitel had that eccentric braid of hair down one shoulder; they reveled in the peculiarity of how they looked. I loved that; for me, it was very freeing.

QUINN: They definitely had quirks that you wouldn't think of as period characters at that time. They even had American accents, and they were playing French!

NAIR: What else did we look at then? Kubrick's *Barry Lyndon*. I remember one scene that was really beautiful between the German woman and Ryan O'Neal.

QUINN: It's a very tender scene.

Production Design

NAIR: I respected Kubrick's pace in that scene, because he let it unfold. That taught me a lot actually. Even though we were going for a much more zany, quicker pace with our film. The humanity of that scene stayed with me and was what we tried to achieve in *Vanity Fair*. Another movie we watched was *Time of the Gypsies*. We always watch that one because of the pagan quality of the fire and water that Kusturica created. We didn't want the straight-laced, uptightness of the Victorian era in this film. In some ways it was the foundation for the aesthetic feasibility of the film, especially in costume and also decor, because the costumes had to work with the decor. It was all about a vibrant world, not a puritanical, straight-laced world.

QUINN: I think elements of *Time of the Gypsies* did make it into the film in terms of dusk, and river, and fire, and those more pagan elements are in that Vauxhall sequence, in a good way.

QUINN: The film evolved a lot as you made it. The characters and the zaniness came about during the filming or in rehearsals. We started to realize that there were funnier bits to include. I remember we were focused on Becky's story but you always wanted to keep the other characters alive, keep their arc going, but then as you met the actors you would kind of fall in love with them. Once you fall in love with an actor's version of a role, then you want to make them bigger in film. That's a really great instinct because you see the charisma and the chemistry they have, so it's only going to be good for the film. Dobbin is the character I'm thinking of right now. He

Declan Quinn, director of photography, and Mira Nair, on location in England during the filming of *Vanity Fair*.

Production Design

The Duellists

The Duellists

was a dry kind of character at first, and then he kind of blossomed into this—

NAIR: [interposing] multi-wigged. Multi-get-up, as we say in Bombay!

QUINN: He's the "Hulk" in the movie, with his hair blowing in the Indian desert.

NAIR: A big training for me in making each character distinctive was *Monsoon Wedding*. We had the same number of actors, sixty-eight to be precise, and making them all separate and equal was a huge lesson from that film.

CINEMATOGRAPHY

NAIR: The other thing I found in my early notes to everybody was to maximize the exteriors and move as many interior scenes to the big exteriors. Then when we were shooting a big exterior like Vauxhall or outside a mansion or on the streets of Mayfair or Brussels we would have the time and money to fully exploit that exterior. Like Amelia and George in the scene when they are reaching to each other and entering Brussels, remember, that was an interior dressing room scene where she says, "Must we go? We don't know anybody," and he says, "Becky

has done so much for us," etc. We put that in the pre-Brussels scene because you and I wanted to give more splendor and stature to their arrival in Brussels. We didn't have the budget to do a splendor and stature one-shot deal, which would take us a whole day and night to do.

QUINN: It was important to have an authenticity to the exteriors, and in order to do that, we needed the depth of the characters and the believability of the dirt and texture and the type of people that would be around, especially in Brussels. Brussels was a big challenge, because we needed to have a sense of them getting ready to fight Napoleon, and the aftermath, and we didn't have the money to do that on the scale that was called for. So the creative way to evoke that was to add that scene in dusk when George and Amelia are walking to the hall, and to get a sense of depth and texture around that, as if you're in a different place. It was important to feel like you were in a different country. Then, selective use of the aftermath of the battlefield, with an overhead shot of the graveyards, gave us scale, but something that we could manage.

NAIR: Going from that big visual expanse and cutting to the intimate visual detail was always a big part of my thinking, both with shooting and cutting the film.

Time of the Gypsies

Pyaasa

Since Becky Sharp sings her way to the top of English society, I looked forward to creating lush song sequences for *Vanity Fair*. A big inspiration was always Guru Dutt, one of the great directors of Indian cinema, who taught me how to maximize the blending of music and image. We looked at his masterpiece, *Pyaasa* (Thirst), for his luminous filming of Waheeda Rehman, before we filmed Becky singing "Now Sleeps the Crimson Petal."

LIGHTING

QUINN: *Vanity Fair* is full of daring costumes and brave hair and locations chosen for their mix of colors, patterns, and architectural details. When you imagine these ornately costumed characters in these ornate rooms and grand halls, you have a deeply textured film. I chose, however, not to be "ornate" with the lighting. I avoided strong cross light and backlight that can be very beautiful but often distracts from what the actors are doing. The light still needed to be beautiful but as natural as possible. Light came from windows in the day and candles at night. I paid a lot of attention to the light on the actor's faces; that it was natural and that we could read their eyes. I want the pho-

tography in a film to move the story along while capturing a mood that supports the emotions of a scene. In *Vanity Fair* we cover huge time spans. There are time jumps from a few weeks to several years throughout the film. In order to get this sense of the passage of time we made sure to have very different ambience and color from one scene to the next. Of course seasonal changes were the best way to show the passage of time, from a bright sunny room, feeling airy and confident, to a gray dusk in autumn, giving a sense of uncertainty or foreboding.

LOCATIONS

NAIR: The locations always informed us how to shoot the scene; the shot design always started from what the location gave us along with the intent of the scene.

QUINN: We both look for the visual strengths of a location, whether it's a room or an exterior. Sometimes we don't get to see it dressed or built until the day we show up. So we have to be able to go in there and decide on the day we shoot what the strong angles are. Even though we may have an idea already, sometimes we have to keep an open mind to change if something better comes along.

Production Design

INDIA

NAIR: And then you should also talk about the heat with which we did India because first we had the challenge of not going to India. We've done a lot of work in India together and we know that so well that I would say, "hot-like," and you would know exactly what I meant.

QUINN: The quarry in England that we used for shooting the India scenes had sandpipers, some sort of birds, nesting in it, so it had this very natural feel. We used that as a backdrop; then we had fifty or seventy-five yards of sand in the foreground, and we put our actors out in the middle of that and used very long lenses. We used propane heat bars with gas under the lens to create the heat haze, and shot a little bit of slow motion to slow the haze down, so it felt believable. And then we had Anu, your lovely assistant, out there in her beautiful Rajasthani garb.

NAIR: The desert beauty!

QUINN: And that worked quite well as a point of view for Dobbin writing in a tent, and we shot Dobbin in the back of Chatham docks and created a similar kind of hot light.

NAIR: You sold the hot light of India brilliantly, even though we were sweating in Colchester. Creating the light difference between India and England was important; then we finally went to India for the finale and shot scenes in the same hot light.

QUINN: It's fun to totally re-create something and to make it work.

NAIR: But you can only do it, I think, truthfully, if you know what it is.

QUINN: That's true. You have to experience it.

SLAVE DANCE

QUINN: The slave dance was you putting Bollywood into *Vanity Fair*, right?

NAIR: This was about the swirl of *Vanity Fair*, about the Lord Steynes of this world who didn't spare any extravagance to create new sensations. All sorts of impressions of the Orient—whether it be slavery or Bedouin musicians—would be served up as a newly tantalizing concoction to entertain the aristocracy. With due respect to Thackeray, it came from a scene in the slave charades. They talked at length about the Bedouins, black slaves, harems, and the English ladies of the court playing charades from the *Arabian Nights*. So it originated from there; making a dance instead would be far more fun, less static than standing in a room sprouting words, and it would give me the chance to do something flamboyant. I took the liberty of a dance, but based on these customs of the times. Then we looked at those paintings, remember, all those Odalisques by Ingres? I thought since I am really imposing my own sensibility to this look of India-English society, why not go all the way? And so in *Vanity Fair* I asked Farah to do that number. It was a huge challenge for Reese because of her pregnancy. I was so amazed that in twelve minutes she learned the dance and was really, really good at it.

QUINN: It was scheduled early in the filming because of the pregnancy. She still had her dexterity and her strengths. And also, wardrobe-wise, they made a black, tight-fitting costume that somehow erased the bump—

NAIR: It did indeed. It was very important to use the dance to tell the story, to speak about the whole tapestry of society at that time. It was about Lady Steyne's shock at the

lascivious sexuality of that dance, Steyne's pleasure at being the one in control, and Rawdon in agony about his wife exhibiting herself and being disgusted and leaving. Then his brother Pitt and Lady Jane were at first surprised, then embarrassed to see Rawdon's humiliation. All these different details were actually of equal importance. It was about not just presenting a spectacle, but forwarding the story with some degree of wit. And, of course, Richard McCabe as the King was a pure brilliant fruitcake.

QUINN: We ended up with an interior that had a tented-in feeling, but still a sense that it was built in a room. Ambient light from candles gave it a richness.

NAIR: The opulence of Eastern splendor. A kind of Orientalist view, like a British view of what they thought the Indian harems, or the Middle Eastern harems, were like.

QUINN: We had to be able to turn around quickly in all of that, so being on a sound stage was very helpful; we had lights on a bong outside so we could pull down the fabric of the walls wherever we needed it to push light through.

NAIR: I remember Douglas Hodge [the actor who plays Pitt Crawley] came up to me that one day and he said, "I've worked in Shepperton Studios for twenty years, and coming in today, and seeing these two young Asian women [Mira Nair & Farah Khan, the choreographer] directing this whole caboodle, I said to myself, 'Something is finally right with England.'"

Choreographer Farah Khan, in white, with Mira Nair, far right and Reese Witherspoon, center, on the Slave Dance set.

Ellipsis at the Core: Editing

Every film is transformed during the editing process and *Vanity Fair* is no exception. Editing involves a close collaboration between editor and director to determine the flow of the film and how the story will ultimately be told. *Vanity Fair* was cut by Allyson Johnson, who also edited Mira Nair's *Monsoon Wedding*.

Part of Johnson's focus was to make sure that the secondary characters in the story didn't get lost in the many subplots while, at the same time, never letting the movie wander too far away from Becky.

Two specific scenes in the movie are good examples of the work that went into editing the movie. The first involved the subplot of the relationship between Amelia and Dobbin. "Dobbin was always thinking of Amelia and I wanted to plant the seed of her longing, too," explains Nair. "We dissolved from her face to Dobbin in India thinking about her, as if their thoughts were mingling. We wanted to show, as Thackeray wrote, that they were both longing for what each of them could not have."

Johnson says this was accomplished in a sort of pseudo-documentary style. While Amelia's letter is being narrated, the film shows the essence of what she is saying but not the actual events. Instead, we get an impressionistic picture of the entire situation between Amelia, her son, and old Osborne. "Ellipsis becomes the core of it," says Johnson. This montage provides a lot of information in a minimum amount of time. "In the space of about sixty seconds, we cut through months of time, travel between India and England, and link up a lot of the story," says Nair. "It's the whole cycle of life in about a minute."

Another interesting edit was the sequence where Becky sings "The Crimson Petal" at Lord Steyne's house. In this sequence, Becky is actually accepted into society and the idea was to show how this happened while she is singing. Even though there is a lot of music in the movie, Nair claims that "this scene was the jewel among them."

Becky enters the room dressed in a black gown while all the other ladies are wearing white. "We start with an overhead crane shot and see all these women in white and red clustered around the drawings," says Nair. "In comes the black swan and the cluster scatters. Becky

tries to join the cluster but is snubbed. Allyson's challenge was to create the sense of Becky's voice being the web that brings everybody together.

"Moment by moment each woman looks at Becky and thinks about allowing her into the group," Johnson explains. "Also, Lord Steyne enters the room at a peak moment in the song so that, when he opens the door, there is a rush of music. There is actually very little dialogue in that scene, besides the song, and so it is more about body language and eyes. There are tears in Reese's eyes and the same in Lady Steyne's. Not a teardrop falling out of the eye, just that glassy look that was so wonderful to capture; you only needed a moment of it."

The scene echoed one of Mira Nair's favorite lines from the Thackeray novel. "When Lady Steyne says, 'I've seen enough cruelty in this house not to want to inflict it,' she makes us feel the ancientness of her suffering, her grief, and her brutalization by this man in her gilded cage," says Nair. "She is moved by Becky's song and the scene says so many things at one time."

Iconic Imagery: Creating the Title Design

*T*o create the title sequence that opens the film, Mira Nair turned to Jakob Trollback and Joe Wright of the New York based graphics firm, Trollback and Company. Nair had worked with Trollback and Company on most of her films including Monsoon Wedding and Hysterical Blindness (for which they won an Emmy for Best Title Design.) Their unique vision, which consists of bold iconic images emerging from a pure black background (see pages 76 to 77), took about two months to conceive and two weeks to execute. The team sat down together on a recent afternoon to talk about the evolution of their ideas and the process by which they created the film's unique title sequence.

MIRA NAIR: I remember calling Jakob from London and talking about the iconic moment in the novel *Vanity Fair* when Becky Sharp throws the book, *Johnson's Dictionary*, at the feet of Miss Pinkerton. I had this idea that we could throw the book and then, out of the dictionary, would pour these words that could become our titles. We even wrote that into the first draft of the film, knowing that it would be too overtly literary to actually do. But that gave us the themes of the film because the words we chose were "ambition, vanity, greed, money . . ."

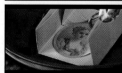

JAKOB TROLLBACK: On a separate but parallel track, Joe had the idea of having images coming out of black.

JOE WRIGHT: It seemed very powerful, and a little bit mysterious at the same time. The black created this nice environment to introduce these elements and also to create a very strong graphic.

TROLLBACK: I don't remember the words that we discussed but we wrote them down, and I started to feel like this could be a poem, maybe a visual poem—

NAIR: And then when you came to see the director's cut, months later, and we had our first conceptual meeting, Joe said, "You know the one thing I keep thinking about from the film is the wealth of detail, the little moments." And then we got the idea of taking icons from the visual details of the film and linking them to the themes we had discussed.

WRIGHT: We explored quite a few different directions with these titles but, straight away, we all gravitated towards the one with a simplicity that would speak in a very pure language. The idea of all these things coming out of black space created a very rich texture, which was in keeping with the film.

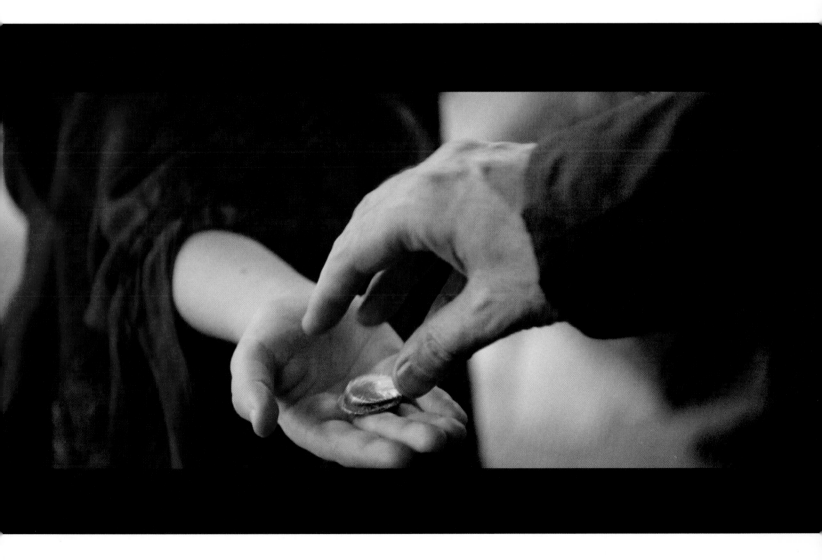

a Mira Nair film

Reese Witherspoon

VANITY *fair*

Eileen A

Jim Broadbent

Gabriel Byrne

Romola Garai

Bob Ho

Rhys Ifans

Geraldine McEwan

Jonathan Rhys Meyers

NAIR: Then you asked me to send the images from the film which we could build on. . .

TROLLBACK: I was not just interested in going through the film and picking out images. What was important was for you, as the director, to find the key elements and icons in the film.

NAIR: For me it was to speak about what Thackeray intended and what I gleaned from the novel; about money and how money changes the equation, about vanity, beauty, mystery and Orientalism. About living and dying, and natural elements; water, specifically, because we were using a lot of natural elements in the film to define passages of time. And then when I sent you those icons we decided, collectively, that we wouldn't repeat images from the film.

TROLLBACK: And then, the question was: How do we create something utterly new but resonant with the film? For me, I wanted this to be kind of a tour de force of an opening sequence . . .

NAIR: Speaking about vanity, greed, and ambition!

TROLLBACK: I had this vanity, I was going to say, that this was going to be something that went into the history books. So I was looking at these images and thinking we needed some magical transitions; some sense of "now you see it, now you don't. . ."

NAIR: The sham and the façade, which were the keys of the film.

TROLLBACK: We did all these experiments shooting through glass, mirrors, and veils. I remember I was look-

ing at window displays and seeing reflections of the street. Sometimes the reflections seemed to cross the boundary of what was actually inside of the store. . .

WRIGHT: Well, I was never really buying it. . .

TROLLBACK: No Joe was like, "We don't need this." And the funny thing was that we actually did shoot mirrored stuff and there were some moments that looked pretty cool but we really didn't get it. All of the effects we tried to do seemed to cheapen the whole thing.

WRIGHT: For me, it was trying too hard. Personally, I shy away from stuff that's too over-the-top. Sometimes that works if the movie is very effects driven but it didn't make sense for *Vanity Fair*. If you can use a very clean and simple form, it doesn't need a lot of trickery. These images sit on this black space, with a real beauty to them.

TROLLBACK: I don't think people are necessarily going to be watching the title sequence and thinking that these are metaphors from the film. They will start to understand the icons in retrospect.

NAIR: It should feel like dream imagery of themes that will later become resonant.

The filmmakers decided not to use images from the film for the opening credits. Instead, they shot images that represented the major themes that play throughout *Vanity Fair*.

Amplifying the Frame:
Producing a Mira Nair Film

*P*roducing films with Mira is always a creative adventure and our work has taken us around the world to incredible places including Mississippi; Uganda; Cuba; Miami; Bayonne, New Jersey; and all over India. Mira creates an extended family wherever she goes. She is an artist with a passionate soul, a unique vision, and a social appetite that knows no limit!

We have always made our films with a fiercely independent spirit, and on *Vanity Fair* we creatively embraced the challenges of shooting a deep period film that demanded scope and intensity. For many of the scenes that give the film its distinction, we had to concoct very creative approaches. Whenever we couldn't achieve a scene within our constraints we would say, "How can we re-conceive this scene in a way that will be more exciting or more interesting than our first idea?"

Vauxhall Gardens, which is a signature set in the novel, was one of our biggest challenges. We imagined elaborate set pieces with special effects, elephants, and a cast of thousands all shooting at night. But faced with a staggering price tag, Mira, Declan, Maria, and Beatrix went to

Producing a Mira Nair Film

work and created a different approach, which became the colorful frolicking picnic that merges into the evening world of exotic theatre. It works very elegantly and effectively to dramatize the presence of the colonized cultures being imported by English society.

Our other two producers, Janette Day and Donna Gigliotti, who spent years developing *Vanity Fair*, found a great match for the material with Mira. Not very often has this period of English society been portrayed from the perspective of a director who grew up surrounded by post-colonial culture.

Thackeray had a great fascination with India and the changes that were happening in England as a result of the wealth created by exploiting the colonies.

Just as Thackeray could hold up a mirror to who we are as people, Mira's subversive vision exposes the universality of human emotion and the need for love.

—Lydia Dean Pilcher, producer

LEFT: Mira Nair, left, with producer Lydia Pilcher in the blue city of Jodhpur while shooting the final scenes of *Vanity Fair*.
ABOVE: Producers Lydia Pilcher, left, and Janette Day.

Breaking the Coconut:
The Mahurat or Opening Ceremony

On the first day of production for each of her movies, Mira Nair performs an opening ceremony called the "Mahurat" (meaning "Auspicious Beginning") for the entire cast and crew. The ceremony begins with a silver tray on which Nair places a fresh coconut, red vermillion paste, rice, and some traditional Indian sweetmeats. She breaks the coconut and everyone eats a small piece. Then, everyone receives a dab of tikka paste between their eyebrows; all the equipment is similarly marked. "It is a very democratic ceremony," says Nair, "we bless everyone and everything involved in the production, from the movie stars to the camera to the dolly tracks to the chairs. Everything is equally important. If the carpenter didn't make the chair, where would the movie star sit?" Shooting starts immediately after the ceremony is completed.

YOGA ON SET

Yoga is part and parcel of Nair's filmmaking; it figures prominently on the daily call sheet for one hour before the shooting day begins. Iyengar yoga teachers are part of the crew, and adjust to the often unusual settings each shooting day would bring. Chapels, barns, hotel rooms, and empty rooms in mansions all come in useful for the daily yoga class. "It genuinely promotes a sense of calm and egolessness on set, besides keeping us strong and focused," says Declan Quinn, the director of cinematography and fellow yogi.

Yoga's discipline of physical flexibility is, for Nair, also a lesson in intellectual flexibility as a director. "The way the body is asked to be in those positions really teaches you the art of resistance and surrender," she says. "If the solutions aren't coming from one place, you have to look at another—which is one of the great lessons a director should always remember." The concentration yoga fosters is also a huge help to counter the stress of production. "I work very hard to prepare people around me," says Nair. "So when we're actually shooting, my work is to preserve that space in myself which operates on instinct. So at that moment of filming, when all engines are go, when all the input is given and is right there in front of you, and it's 'Action!'—then you know it's your only chance. Then I must not operate with the stress of pressure or ego. It's about instinct. And with yoga, the space for instinct has grown."

LEFT: Max Keene, first assistant director, looks on as Drew Kunin, sound recordist, and Mira Nair practice *Utkatasana* in Queen's Woods at Hatfield while filming the escape from Brussels scene. Photo by Sooni Taraporevala.

VANITY*fair*

The Illustrated Screenplay

EXT. THE DOCKS. LONDON 1802. EVE.

In a sordid part of the docks, a nobleman's carriage draws to a halt. Boys taunt the coachman and the postilions who jump down to open the door. A tall man with a face of stone emerges, the Marquess of Steyne. He looks up at a lighted window and picks his way carefully towards the entrance.

INT. SHARP'S STUDIO. EVE.

This is the studio of Francis Sharp. With his hard-drinking group he laughs at a puppet show performed from behind a dirty curtain. The marionettes represent a pot-bellied, dissipated nobleman, an equally raddled old harridan and a young girl. An unseen child mimics their voices.

> VOICE
>
> "Is this your daughter, madame? I will take her, half the cash down and half in consuls."
>
> "Surely, mama, you will not sell me to the highest bidder though he is a lord!"
>
> "Why ever not, child? We cannot flout the rules of Good Society."

The general laugh is interrupted with a cough.

> STEYNE
>
> Is this an inconvenient moment?

The company turns to see the immaculate nobleman. They try to scramble to their feet. He takes in the drunken Sharp.

> STEYNE
>
> I have returned for another look, Mr Sharp. . . but I can always come back another time. . . .

> SHARP
>
> No need, my lord. There it is. *Virtue Betrayed*. One of my best. Look as long as you want.

He attempts to stand which is beyond him and instead waves towards a painting of a beautiful woman who is pulling a shawl around herself as she recoils from the indistinct figure of a man. It is a wonderful piece of work.

> STEYNE
>
> And the price?

> SHARP
>
> Four guineas, my lord. Just as I said. They're all four guineas.

> BECKY (V.O.)
>
> Not that one! That one is ten!

From behind the curtain steps a little girl. She is very pretty but the look in her eyes is older than her years.

> BECKY
>
> *Virtue Betrayed* is ten guineas.

> STEYNE
>
> It is too much, little miss.

> BECKY
>
> Good.

Steyne turns to Sharp who shrugs.

> SHARP
>
> The model was my late wife. The child doesn't want to part with it.

Steyne is, if anything, intrigued by the girl.

> STEYNE
>
> And if I pay ten guineas for this picture of your mother, will you be happy then to see it go?

> BECKY
>
> No. But it will be too much to refuse.

There is something moving in the child's solemnity.

> STEYNE
>
> Very well. Ten it shall be.

Taking some gold coins from his pocket, he counts them into Sharp's eager hand. With a bow to the child, he takes up the picture and walks away. Sharp whispers.

> *SHARP*
>
> *Good, child. You're learning.*

She answers disdainfully.

> *BECKY*
>
> *I would rather have kept it.*

The following pages include the entire screenplay for *Vanity Fair*. As in every movie, several cuts were made during the final edit of the film. To highlight these alterations, deleted pieces of dialogue and scenes are italicized and printed in gray for easy reference.

But she stands, impassive, as the portrait of her dead mother is being carried off.

INT. ANTE ROOM. MISS PINKERTON'S ACADEMY. CHISWICK. DAY.

Becky, in black mourning, walks between two black skirts down a long corridor. Servants brush past them, the clanging and banging of a working household are all around.

WOMAN IN BLACK
The orphanage can take her but I thought you might find her useful. With both parents dead, there's no one to fuss. You can do what you like with the child.

MISS PINKERTON
She's very small.

WOMAN IN BLACK
But strong enough. She'll work long hours.

MISS PINKERTON
Hmm. One wrong step and she's out in the street. How fluent is her French?

WOMAN IN BLACK
Very. Her mother was Parisian.

There is a whispered addendum to this which we do not hear.

Fashions change, architecture changes, but what compels human beings to love and to live doesn't really change. Technologically we may have advanced beyond our wildest expectations but we're still the same sexual and social animals we've always been. What Thackeray did brilliantly was to hold up a mirror to who we are as people, not just to the society that he was writing about then. What makes the story classic and contemporary is because he was writing in a truthful and really profound way about the universality of human emotion and human longing, within a social context that will never change. —Gabriel Byrne

MISS PINKERTON
I see. Well, the less said about *that* the better.

The camera pulls back as the child, flanked by the two black crow-like women, walks towards her future.

INT. MISS PINKERTON'S HALL. 1814. DAY

A young woman, Becky Sharp, 19, sweeps the floor. A teacher in severe clothing walks into the corridor, berating her.

TEACHER
You've tidied the library?

BECKY
(beginning to untie her apron)
Yes, Miss Green.

TEACHER
And the sheet music? It's all put away?

BECKY
(taking her apron off)
It is, Miss Green.

TEACHER
What about the study hall? You've swept it thoroughly?

BECKY
(throwing the apron down)
I have—and for the last time!

TEACHER
Don't be too sure, Miss Sharp. Life can be very unpredictable.

Becky Sharp pauses for a moment.

BECKY
Oh, I do hope so, Miss Green!

And, throwing down her apron, she turns and sweeps out of the hallway.

EXT. MISS PINKERTON'S ACADEMY. 1814. DAY.

The door opens and out steps Becky, 19, a beauty with the eyes of a fox. As a coachman loads a smart trunk labelled "A.S." onto the vehicle, another young lady, Amelia Sedley, is bidding good-bye to their headmistress, Miss Pinkerton, who carries two copies of Johnson's dictionary.

MISS PINKERTON

Goodbye, Miss Sedley. You are a credit to us. Take this copy of the great Dr Johnson's dictionary as a token of our good wishes.

Amelia hugs her friends goodbye as Becky descends the stairs.

MISS PINKERTON

Miss Sharp, I can't pretend to understand why you prefer the post of a country governess to your position here.

BECKY

Can you not, Miss Pinkerton?

MISS PINKERTON

But I suppose I must accept your decision.

BECKY

Yes. I suppose you must, Miss Pinkerton.

MISS PINKERTON

And you feel quite ready to leave us?

BECKY

Chaque esclave veut s'echapper s'il peut, vache bete.

The subtitles read, "Every slave wants to escape if he can, you stupid cow."

MISS PINKERTON

I am glad to hear it. Then good day to you, Miss Sharp.

As they climb into the carriage. A thought strikes Becky.

BECKY

Am I not to have my Johnson's dictionary?

Miss Pinkerton hesitates. Reluctantly, she hands it over.

MISS PINKERTON

Very well. Here you are. Treat it as a symbol of the education we have given you.

She nods and steps back. The horses move as Becky answers.

BECKY

I certainly will, Miss Pinkerton!

She hurls the book from the coach to land at the feet of Miss Pinkerton. As it hits the ground, a shower of words explodes from it: Ambition, Ingenuity, Charm, Manipulation, Courage, Cunning, Endurance, Duplicity, Mendacity, Tenacity. To the sound of Becky's laughter, the carriage rolls away.

INT. COACH. DAY.

Amelia is truly shocked but Becky couldn't be less repentant.

BECKY

Silly old trout. She doesn't know a word of French though she's too proud to admit it. *Vive la France! Vive Napoleon!*

AMELIA

Becky, how can you be so wicked and vengeful?

BECKY

And why not? In all the years I spent there I only ever knew kind words from you. Revenge may be wicked but it's perfectly natural.

AMELIA

Perhaps it is . . . Oh, but you're wrong to make me say such things!

The Good Girl envies the other's free-thinking.

BECKY

Never mind that. Let's talk of how we're to spend my precious week of freedom. My first priority is to form an opinion of Captain Osborne. I take that duty very seriously, you know.

AMELIA

It will not tax you. George is quite perfect.

BECKY

So he should be. None but the perfect deserve my Amelia.

AMELIA

You will love him and he will love you.

BECKY

And your parents? I confess I'm a little nervous of them. . . . You'll correct me if I step out of turn.

AMELIA

Be yourself and everyone will love you. I do.

BECKY

Tell me more about your brother.

AMELIA

Jos? There's nothing to add to what you already know. He's home on leave from India.

BECKY

What is his job again?

AMELIA

He's the Collector of Boggley Wollah.

BECKY

Is that good?

AMELIA

Well, it has made him rich but I'm afraid his life is lonely. If only he was married. Becky? Whatever is the matter with you?

But she knows and the two girls dissolve into giggles.

INT. SEDLEY DINING ROOM. RUSSELL SQUARE.

Joseph Sedley is a large and ungainly dandy. He eats *con gusto.* Behind Jos's chair is his Indian servant, Biju, whom the other footmen eye warily. Becky and Amelia, ravishing in evening dress, and her parents make up the party.

MRS SEDLEY

And what children exactly are to have the benefit of your instruction, Miss Sharp?

BECKY

The daughters of Sir Pitt Crawley of Queen's Crawley, ma'am. He is among the first gentlemen of Hampshire. Or so I was told when I applied for the position.

MRS SEDLEY

Hmm. He is not so prominent that we have ever heard of him.

SEDLEY

Do you know the county at all?

BECKY

No, but that does not frighten me. I love to visit new places.

JOSEPH

Really?

BECKY

Oh, indeed! How I envy men who can explore for themselves all the wonders of the world!

JOSEPH

Should you like to visit India, do you think?

BECKY

India! I cannot think of anywhere I would rather see! The palaces of Delhi, the Taj Mahal, the Burning Ghats . . .

Mrs Sedley looks at her husband and rolls her eyes.

SEDLEY

Have you made a study of India, Miss Sharp?

BECKY

Not as much as I would like. I am enraptured by every scent and flavour of the East!

SEDLEY

Its flavours can be rather hot.

I think that Becky Sharp is a really modern heroine trapped in the wrong century; she was feisty and difficult and different for the time. She lived during a time in British history where there was much change. People were going to the colonies and bringing back new influences.

I think the influence of the Becky character is far reaching; Margaret Mitchell based Scarlett O'Hara on Becky Sharp.

If Becky was alive now she'd be running ICI or be in government and no one would think twice about the way she is. She is someone who does what she needs to do in order to survive.

—Janette Day, producer

BECKY

But so romantic! Do you remember how the Princess put pepper on the cream tarts in The Arabian Nights*? I think there is no Eastern delight that I should shrink from!*

MRS SEDLEY

Joseph, you heard Miss Sharp. Let her try your curry. Joseph has lost his taste for English food, Miss Sharp, and I indulge him when he's here.

JOSEPH

Indeed you do, Mama. But I wonder if the taste is not too foreign for Miss Sharp.

BECKY

Oh, I know I will like anything that comes from India!

Mrs Sedley is more than equal to the game Becky is playing.

JOSEPH

Gad, if you think so! Biju! Fetch a plate!

AMELIA

Do be careful, Becky. Those curries can burn.

MRS SEDLEY

Let Miss Sharp try it if she wants to, dear.

Biju brings a plate which Joseph heaps with curry and then takes it to Becky. She snatches up a large green chili on the top and lays it on her tongue with a dashing glance at Joseph. She bites and swallows. Her face explodes. Tears start into her eyes. Mrs Sedley is enjoying herself.

MRS SEDLEY

So, Miss Sharp, how do you find your first taste of India?

But Becky is not easily defeated. Conquering her flaming tongue, she wipes her streaming eyes and deliberately takes a heaped spoonful of the fiery stew, pausing only to gasp:

BECKY

Delicious!

Joseph gives a triumphant look to his mother.

INT. DRAWING ROOM. SEDLEY HOUSE. EVE.

Becky is singing while Amelia accompanies her. Jos, who has been alternately admiring Becky and guzzling sweetmeats, applauds wildly. Mrs Sedley is more contained.

JOSEPH

My word, Miss Sharp. You've the voice of an angel in Heaven.

MRS SEDLEY

Yes. You must have some lessons, my dear.

But if Becky is offended by this jibe, she does not show it. An officer, William Dobbin, slips in. Amelia has not noticed him and he puts his finger to his lips to silence the others. He is free to admire the face of Amelia until she spies him, breaks off and jumps to her feet.

AMELIA

Captain Dobbin, is George not with you?

MRS SEDLEY

Yes. Where is my dear godson?

DOBBIN

Pray don't concern yourselves. George sends his regrets. Work holds him prisoner tonight.

AMELIA

But he's coming to the picnic at Vauxhall tomorrow? Do please say he is.

DOBBIN

He wouldn't miss it for worlds.

Becky watches Dobbin curiously while Jos only looks at her.

To make these waistcoats for a man of his size and dignity took at least a day, part of which he employed in hiring a servant to wait upon him and his native; and in instructing the agent who cleared his baggage, his boxes, his books, which he never read; his chests of mangoes, chutney, and currie-powders; his shawls for presents to people whom he didn't know as yet; and the rest of his Persicos apparatus. —William Makepeace Thackeray, *Vanity Fair*, 1847

INT. SEDLEY DINING ROOM/HALLWAY. NIGHT.

Mr Sedley sits toiling at the dining room table which is covered in papers and ledgers. Mrs Sedley is at the door.

MRS SEDLEY

Come to bed, now. You must be finished with those boring old numbers.

SEDLEY

If only I could be.

His voice is bitter. With a sigh, he lays down his pen. He is clearly deeply worried, but his wife is thinking of other things and she does not notice how worried he is.

MRS SEDLEY

I wish Jos hadn't planned this silly picnic. It's only to show off all his Indian paraphernalia. He'll drink too much and who knows what he'll say if the little minx works on him.

She has led the way out of the room and onto the staircase.

SEDLEY

Let Jos marry whom he likes. She has no fortune but nor had you. She's beautiful, good-humoured and clever. Better her than a black Mrs Sedley from Boggley Wollah and a dozen mahogany grandchildren. *And she sings well. Grant her that.*

MRS SEDLEY

She sings like a siren. Let's hope Jos can steer clear of the rocks.

She goes into her room.

INT. GAMBLING DEN. DUSK.

Captain George Osborne, handsome as a man can be, is gambling with other louche officers for vast stakes.

GAMBLER

Well, Osborne? Are you in or out?

George hesitates. He is way out of his depth.

GEORGE

I'm in.

The other turns over his cards and sweeps the pool. George swallows his hideous loss as he stands to greet his friend.

GEORGE

Hello, Dobs. How was Amelia?

DOBBIN

Waiting outside, brimming with joy at the prospect of seeing your face.

DOBBIN

George, your Amelia awaits!

George sighs slightly at this.

GEORGE

Ho hum, Dobs. Unflagging devotion is all very well but it does rather take out the challenge . . . Tell me, what was the hanger-on governess like?

EXT. OBELISK & POND. DAY.

Peacocks stroll before a Chinese pavilion. George & Amelia, Becky & Jos approach the centre of the pond at the Obelisk from different directions. The girls hold their dresses up as they step barefoot through the water.

AMELIA

Dearest George, you cannot know how Becky has been longing to meet you.

BECKY

I want to be quite sure that you are good enough for dear Amelia.

She means the remark to be playful but George does not find it so. He stiffens.

GEORGE

And who is to decide? You?

AMELIA

Becky only meant—

JOSEPH

Come, Miss Becky. May I show you the pavilion and the delights I have prepared for us?

Becky is aware that somehow the moment with George has gone wrong but she is grateful to have more catchable quarry.

"Not now, Mr. Sedley," said Rebecca, with a sigh. "My spirits are not equal to it; besides, I must finish the purse. Will you help me, Mr. Sedley?" And before he had time to ask how, Mr. Joseph Sedley, of the East India Company's service, was actually seated tete-a-tete with a young lady, looking at her with a most killing expression; his arms stretched out before her in an imploring attitude, and his hands bound in a web of green silk, which she was unwinding. In this romantic position Osborne and Amelia found the interesting pair, when they entered to announce that tiffin was ready.

—William Makepeace Thackeray, *Vanity Fair*, 1847

I have always loved the image by Thackeray of Jos' hands bound in a web of the green silk with which Becky is making her purse. I know we've lost the whole purse idea, but is there any way at all you can think of including this image? It is so symbolic of the web Becky makes wherever she goes and could be splendidly cinematic.

—E-mail from Mira Nair to Julian Fellowes

BECKY
You may show me *anything you choose*, Mr Sedley.

She slips her arm through Jos's and they move off towards the Pavilion. Amelia takes George's arm.

AMELIA
She was only joking.

GEORGE
I don't care for governesses to joke at my expense.

AMELIA
Don't be so strict. Not when I've missed you as much as I have.

GEORGE
You only saw me last Tuesday.

AMELIA
Then I've missed you since Tuesday.

GEORGE
You little goose.

But he pats her hand on his arm and they stroll on, Dobbin trailing behind them.

EXT. PARK
Biju brings food to the Pavilion, watching his master. He mutters in Hindi to himself. The subtitles read: "He's harder to land than he looks."

INT. CHINESE PAVILION - DAY
The meal is over. As the camera moves there is some curious laughing and wriggling. Joseph comes into view, trussed and bound with purple silk which Becky pretends to roll into a ball but instead loops over and over her victim.

JOSEPH
Miss Sharp, I thought I was to help unravel your silks not to be sold into slavery!

BECKY
Nonsense, Mr Sedley! Stay still, I beg you, or I shall never have it untangled.

But she casts another loop of silk around him. He laughs.

JOSEPH

I surrender. I am your prisoner.

BECKY

You have only to ask and I shall release you.

JOSEPH

But why would I ever want that? Biju! We're ready!

The servant approaches with the Macau on his wrist. Becky seeks to gain him for her cause.

BECKY

Biju! In France your name would make you Mr Sedley's jewel! What does it mean in India?

BIJU

Just Biju.

He gazes at her opaquely. Jos has missed all this, busying himself with taking the bird from Biju's arm.

JOSEPH

Dearest Miss Sharp, I give him to you.

BECKY

What? Your beautiful bird? Oh, I couldn't!

JOSEPH

You say you love everything that comes from India. Take him. He is my ambassador. . . .

Becky is within sight of victory. She holds out her hand for the brilliant bird and he hops obediently onto it.

EXT. RIVERBANK - UNDER A TREE. DAY
George sits with Dobbin and Amelia.

AMELIA

It's so hot.

GEORGE

Figs! Miss Sedley is too hot. Make yourself useful and take her shawl!

AMELIA

I wish you wouldn't call him that.

GEORGE

Why not? Master Figs, the Grocer's Son. That's what you are, ain't it, Figs?

DOBBIN

I am.

AMELIA

Our fathers are only merchants. I cannot see there is much difference.

GEORGE

Can't you? I can.

DOBBIN

Careful, George. I'm used to your high-handed tone but Miss Sedley may not care for it.

GEORGE

She must take me as I am. Either that or leave me and face the world alone.

DOBBIN

She would not be alone for long.

Amelia chooses to take all this as a joke and laughs gaily as Dobbin bows with a smile and, taking the shawl, moves off towards the pavilion. George shrugs off Dobbin's criticism. His attention is taken by Jos and Becky.

GEORGE

I hope Jos isn't getting too deep.

AMELIA

Becky is my friend, dearest George. I should welcome her as a sister. And I hope you would.

Behind them, Dobbin sits in the shade, Amelia's shawl still folded over his arm. He hums the tune that Amelia played and, with a quick glance to make sure he is not being watched, he lifts the shawl gently to his lips . . .

INT. CHINESE PAVILION. DAY
Becky strokes the astonishing plumage.

BECKY

How exotic he is! I wish you would tell me more of your life in India. How many servants do you have?

JOSEPH

Enough to keep a fella tolerably comfortable. What is it, Biju? Thirty? Forty?

Becky looks across and starts to imagine.

BECKY

I cannot think it would be hard to adjust to such a life. . . .

INT. A CHINESE PAVILION. DAY.
Becky lies in the pavilion. Chequered light falls through the latticed windows as Ayahs comb her hair, oil her hands and feet, bring sweetened drinks for her delight . . .

JOSEPH (V.O.)

Not for you, my dear. Never for you. You were born for ease and pleasure. To lie in the shade while a thousand minions minister to your every desire—

GEORGE (V.O.)

Jos!

EXT. BRIDGE AT RIVER BANK. DUSK
Becky walks up the path to the bridge to join Amelia.

AMELIA

Well?

BECKY

He called me "dearest" twice and squeezed my hand and look! He gave me his precious bird.

The gleaming Macau is still on her wrist.

AMELIA

Oh Becky! That is surely a good sign!

BECKY

I know. Feel my heart, how it beats, my dear!

Their eyes stray to the riverbank where George and Jos climb in to one of the boats.

AMELIA

I wish they would come back!

BECKY

Me too!

But the girlish gush has drained from her voice for her instinct tells her that this tete-a-tete bodes ill.

EXT. BOAT. DUSK
George is speaking softly but firmly to the captured Jos.

GEORGE

What are you playing at with the little governess?

JOSEPH

Well, I . . .

GEORGE

Jos, Jos, you've forgotten how these things work! Do you think the fellas down at the club will let their wives dine with a governess? Seriously, Jos, if I'm to marry your sister—

JOSEPH

If?

From the bridge, they are still watched by the women.

AMELIA

What are they talking about? Can you guess?

BECKY

Yes . . . I think I probably can.

As they watch, the boat pulls over on the far bank and Joseph clambers ashore. He looks back at her. George's poison has been ingested. He hurries away. With a squawk the Macau takes to the air and flies across to its master. Becky looks round.

BECKY

Biju?

Where the servant once stood, there is nobody. The picnic has been packed and removed without a trace. Her dream is over.

EXT. LONDON STREET. DAY. RAIN.
Luggage stands in the mud, waiting to be loaded on the Mail Coach. Smart passengers climb inside but the ordinary sit on benches on the roof. Becky is saying goodbye to Amelia.

AMELIA

Oh Becky, who knows? It may turn out a blessing in disguise.

BECKY

The disguise is very convincing.

But she gives Amelia a squeeze. It's not her fault. Becky hesitates for a moment then she takes a small package from the hand luggage she is carrying.

BECKY

Here. This is for you.

Amelia opens it to find a small painting.

BECKY

It's one of my father's . . . I've nothing else to give.

AMELIA

Becky, I couldn't.

BECKY

Take it. I want you to have it. At least I know it'll be safe with you.

She turns to get on the coach. Becky is the last passenger to climb aboard. She takes hold of the ladder.

AMELIA

Couldn't I pay for a seat inside?

BECKY

They're all taken. But don't worry. I prefer the open air.

The coachman cracks his whip. The journey begins.

EXT. COACH. DAY.

The rain lashes down drenching Becky. The coach stops by a pair of gates topped with stone beasts. The gates, like the house, were once magnificent. They are not magnificent now.

COACHMAN

This is Queen's Crawley.

Becky climbs down as her battered trunk is thrown after her. The coach drives on. She takes a handle and starts to drag her trunk through the puddles towards the building.

EXT. QUEEN'S CRAWLEY. EVE.

Wet and weary, Becky arrives at the vast house. She takes the bell pull and tugs. There are shuffling sounds and with a squeaking hinge the huge door is pulled open by an unshaven old man in a dirty wig and a filthy tailcoat.

OLD MAN

Yes?

BECKY

Can you tell Sir Pitt Crawley that Miss Sharp has arrived. And bring in my trunk if you please.

She would go past him but he blocks her path.

OLD MAN

Miss Sharp?

BECKY

Yes. Miss Sharp. Governess to your master's children. Now will you kindly let me pass.

OLD MAN

Certainly. But as for my telling Sir Pitt, there's no need.

BECKY

Why not?

OLD MAN

You've already told him yourself.

Becky Sharp is one of the greatest female characters written in literature, and Reese has wit, intelligence, guile, an enticing quality and that fantastic appeal that makes an actor a movie star. Becky Sharp is a complicated character; I wanted to preserve her complexity, her ambition, her folly, yet I wanted the audience to go with her. It's no fun seeing a movie where you hate the protagonist. Reese's particular impish appeal, her foxiness, her exquisite comic timing, her ability to acutely read the human heart—this is what made her Becky Sharp irresistible. —Mira Nair

Laughing raucously at Becky's discomfort, he seizes the trunk and closes the door.

INT. GREAT HALL. QUEEN'S CRAWLEY. EVE.

The Great Hall is huge, dirty and uncomfortable. In the window is a table covered with books, ledgers and writs. The company stand round another rough table set before the fire. A couple of countrymen rather than servants in threadbare livery are under Horrocks, the butler. With Becky and Sir Pitt is his middle-aged son, Pitt Crawley, pompous and sleek, as well as two girls, Rose and Celia.

PITT

For these and all Thy other gifts, may the Lord make us truly thankful. Amen.

As they start to sit, a faded woman in her fifties enters and Pitt Crawley stands again. His father does not.

SIR PITT

You haven't met Lady Crawley, my dear. This is the girls' mother.

Becky rises and bobs a little curtsey.

SIR PITT

She's not the mother of my sons. Is she, Pitt? Pitt's mother, my first wife, was the daughter of a lord which makes him grander than all of us put together. Doesn't it, Pitt?

PITT

Whatever you say, Sir.

SIR PITT

Oh yes, she was grand. Too grand for me. This one ain't, though. Her father was an *ironmonger*, wasn't he, my lady?

LADY CRAWLEY

He was, Sir.

Her dignity at his cruelty elicits Becky's sympathy.

BECKY

When shall we discuss the girls' lessons? My strengths are music, drawing and French but I can teach them whatever you wish.

LADY CRAWLEY

You'll be kind to my girls, Miss Sharp? They're very delicate.

Becky jumps and looks down. There is a frog in her lap. Rose and Celia giggle and watch her. She brushes it off.

BECKY

Don't worry. I'll treat them just as sensitively as they deserve.

She gives the girls a look. In truth, they quite like her.

SIR PITT

What is this?

Pitt picks up the ill-written menu card.

PITT

Potage de mouton a l'Ecossaise.

SIR PITT

Mutton broth. What sheep was it, Horrocks, and when did you kill?

HORROCKS

One of the black-faced Scotch, Sir Pitt. We killed on Thursday.

SIR PITT

Did she squeal?

HORROCKS

Didn't she just.

Naturally this rather spoils the soup.

INT. BECKY'S BEDROOM. NIGHT.

Becky is huddled in a four poster, a copy of *The Arabian Nights* open next to her as she writes by candle light.

BECKY (V.O.)

To be honest, dearest Amelia, Sir Pitt is not what you and I think a baronet should be. More ancient stable than ancient fable—

The door opens and there stands the baronet in his filthy dressing gown. He snatches up the candle.

SIR PITT

No lights after eleven, you little hussy. Go to bed in the dark unless you want me to come in for your candle every night.

He blows out the flame and, like Becky, we are in the dark.

INT. SCHOOLROOM. DAY.

Becky is teaching the two girls, watched by Lady Crawley.

BECKY

"I would like to visit London." *"Je voudrais visiter a Londres."* Rose.

But as the child stands to speak her lesson, we hear only the voice of her letter to Amelia.

BECKY (V.O.)

Lady Crawley is a pale cipher and all in all, my hopes for the family lie with Sir Pitt's younger son Captain Rawdon Crawley, who will soon be back from his regiment.

In the room hang two portraits, one of Mr Pitt and one of a dashing officer, Captain Rawdon Crawley.

BECKY

His brother, Mr Pitt Crawley, meanwhile, has the charm of an undertaker and the humour of a corpse.

During this the door opens and Pitt enters.

PITT

Miss Sharp, I thought you might like to see my pamphlet on the Chickasaw tribes.

In my opinion Becky Sharp is this amazing sort of early feminist. She has incredible opinions and ideas about how she was going to raise her social stature through different means of manipulation and social climbing. Though she's been deprived—having no parents and no place to go in the world—still, she manages to succeed. Every success she has in her life is based on her own merit and I think that's a very modern idea for a period film.

—Reese Witherspoon

BECKY

I swear, Mr Crawley, you must be a mind-reader. For there is *no subject* of more interest to me.

She seizes the booklet eagerly. Pitt is pleased. Lady Crawley is possibly more sceptical.

INT. BECKY'S BEDROOM. NIGHT.

She is writing her letter again.

BECKY (V.O.)

You will be happy to hear that I think I've found a way to make myself indispensable to Sir Pitt.

MONTAGE AT QUEEN'S CRAWLEY.

BECKY (V.O.)

There is to be a visitor at Humdrum Hall.

The servants unbag a huge chandelier and wheel a sideboard into the hall, taking orders from Becky.

BECKY (V.O.)

Sir Pitt has a half-sister, as rich as Croesus, whom or should I say *which*, he adores. And now he is all of a dither to make the house ready to receive her. I promise you, dearest Amelia, that by the time I have finished, the old man will have a very proper sense of the merits of his latest employee. I will bring order from chaos and light from darkness.

Becky holds a manual with a diagram of a place setting which she is checking on the central table in the Great Hall. She senses someone's eyes on her and looking up she sees Lady Crawley watching sadly from the stair.

Next, outside the front, a British battle axe, the Countess of Southdown and her gentle daughter, Jane, get out of a carriage. Jane is immediately greeted by Mr Pitt as, accompanied by Becky's voice, they walk inside.

BECKY (V.O.)

We are quite a party. Mr Pitt's intended, Lady Jane Sheepshanks, has arrived with her mother, the old Countess of Southdown, whom Sir Pitt detests.

Becky holds an open fan before the face of Sir Pitt. She flips it away and he is agog. The Great Hall gleams like a palace state chamber, the table is laid with shining silver. On the sideboard shines a stack of gleaming family plate.

BECKY (V.O.)
They say Miss Crawley means to leave her fortune to Captain Rawdon Crawley who will accompany her for the journey.

Finally, she pulls him over to the corner. There is his table of papers, tidy and trim. It is the final detail.

SIR PITT
By Heaven, Miss Becky. We don't deserve you.

INT. SERVANTS' CORRIDOR. QUEEN'S CRAWLEY. DAY.
Mr Pitt is kneeling, leading the servants in prayer.

PITT
Almighty Lord, look down in mercy on these your humble and wretched servants here below—

A door flies open. Sir Pitt strides through their midst.

SIR PITT
Come with me, sir! And remember! No preachifying while she's here!

PITT
But the servants—

SIR PITT
Servants be hanged! You can miss a few prayers to keep a hundred thousand in the family!

He flings a door open and hurries through it followed by his son and leaving the servants in fits of laughter.

EXT/INT. QUEEN'S CRAWLEY. DAY.
A travelling coach arrives at the door. Pitt, who waits with the others inside the hall, isn't finished.

PITT
What is money compared to our immortal souls?

SIR PITT
You mean your brother's going to get it and not you.

This is heard by Lady Southdown who whispers to Jane.

LADY SOUTHDOWN
We'll see about that.

The carriage has stopped. Rawdon Crawley, a handsome guards officer, steps out, giving his hand to Matilda Crawley, a spoiled and crotchety fuss pot. She looks about.

MISS CRAWLEY
I see Pitt's intended is among the guests. They'll be after you to marry next, you wicked boy.

RAWDON
But how could I, Aunt Tilly, when my heart belongs to you?

This is *just* what she likes to hear. Behind them, her self-important maid, Firkin, climbs down from the box.

SIR PITT
Matilda, welcome. You know Lady Southdown, I think. And her daughter, Lady Jane.

Matilda nods curtly. Lady Southdown is miffed.

LADY SOUTHDOWN
That's put us in our place.

LADY JANE
We may have the titles, mama. But Miss Crawley has the money.

LADY SOUTHDOWN
And don't we know it.

PITT
Aunt Matilda, on behalf of the—

MISS CRAWLEY
Keep your toadying 'til I get to a fire. You can suck up all you wish once I'm warm.

The World is a looking-glass, and gives back to every man the reflection of his own face.

—William Makepeace Thackeray, *Vanity Fair*, 1847

She takes Sir Pitt's arm and walks on. Rawdon passes Pitt.

RAWDON
Too bad, old boy. Better luck next time.

Rawdon's attention is taken by the sight of a stranger. . . . He bows with a smile. Sir Pitt stops and turns.

SIR PITT
Now, Miss Becky. This is my younger son, Rawdon, and mind you keep clear of his fluttering lashes. He breaks hearts for a hobby but he's a soldier through and through!

This makes Miss Crawley laugh and even Rawdon smile.

BECKY
I'm warned.

INT. DRAWING ROOM. QUEEN'S CRAWLEY. LATE DAY.
The house party, minus Sir Pitt, are in their finery, attended by Horrocks. Miss Crawley pets a rather irritable lap dog. Becky plays the piano. Rawdon is turning the pages for her. Lady Southdown sighs.

LADY SOUTHDOWN
Queen's Crawley seems even more run down than when I was last here. Mr Crawley will have plenty to do when . . . when the place is his.

RAWDON
You mean Pitt will need Aunt Matilda's money on top of his own inheritance?

He laughs, sharing the joke with Miss Crawley and Becky. Even Lady Jane smiles down at her embroidery.

LADY SOUTHDOWN
That was not my meaning.

MISS CRAWLEY
What was it, then?

RAWDON
Pitt don't mind, do ye, Pitt? Not when the Bible tells us that money's the root of all evil.

PITT
It is not money but the love of money that's at the root of evil.

RAWDON
You mean it's all right to want it as long as you hate it.

This is directed towards Becky who smiles. Which Pitt sees.

RAWDON
You must be as bored as a brick down here.

BECKY
I have your father and brother for company.

RAWDON
Precisely. There are not many laughs in Miss Crawley.

Behind, Pitt has taken a plate from Horrocks's silver tray. He approaches Miss Crawley.

PITT
I seem to remember anchovy paste is a favourite of yours, aunt.

Miss Crawley takes one, sniffs it and calls her dog.

MISS CRAWLEY
Byron!

She feeds the delicacy to the animal. Becky has watched the whole thing and smiles.

BECKY
I don't agree. I suspect she has the quickest wit in the room.

RAWDON
I mean my brother, not my aunt. They called him Miss Crawley at Eton. Go on, admit it. He's the dullest dog in shoe leather.

BECKY
Really, Captain Crawley. Are you trying to steer me towards an indiscretion?

RAWDON
Why? Would you like me to steer you?

BECKY
No man has managed it yet.

She plays on. He drops a folded paper on the keys. Without a pause, Becky holds it in the candle and throws it into a plant pot.

Miss Crawley responds to the halt in the music.

MISS CRAWLEY

What was that?

BECKY

Nothing. A false note.

She laughs at Rawdon's blushes. The girls come dawdling in.

BECKY

Alors, Rose, Celia. Depechez. Faites vos obeissances a votre tante.

RAWDON

Don't waste your time, Miss Sharp. All foreign languages are ancient Greek to my sisters.

BECKY

And always will be if they're not spoken before them.

MISS CRAWLEY

I quite agree, Miss Sharp. What a treat to find someone cultured in this house! And how unlikely! Vous parlez bien.

Becky stops playing, leaves Rawdon and comes over.

BECKY

My mother was French.

MISS CRAWLEY

A French mother? That is altogether too romantic for a governess! Who was she?

BECKY

Have you heard of the Montmorencys?

MISS CRAWLEY

Who has not? So you are an impoverished aristocrat. Pity. I had you down for an adventuress.

She laughs wickedly. Becky has got her measure.

BECKY

And are they mutually exclusive?

MISS CRAWLEY

Please tell me there's *something* disreputable in your past.

BECKY

Well . . . my father was an artist.

MISS CRAWLEY

Ah, that's better. A starving one, I hope.

BECKY

Ravenous.

They are distracted by the arrival of Sir Pitt.

SIR PITT

Who's ravenous? Besides me. Horrocks? When's dinner?

HORROCKS

Any minute now, Sir Pitt.

BECKY

I'd best excuse myself. Come along, girls.

MISS CRAWLEY

Is Miss Sharp not to dine with us?

SIR PITT

Don't ask me, ask Pitt.

MISS CRAWLEY

Nephew? I hope she is not banished in my honour. You know I am nothing if not democratic.

This is almost too much for Pitt but Jane murmurs to him.

JANE

It's no great sacrifice in the cause of peace.

He nods and pats her arm. She does know how to manage him.

PITT

Of course Miss Sharp will dine with us if you wish it, Aunt.

A shabby footman arrives and whispers in Horrocks's ear.

HORROCKS

Dinner is served.

The party rises and moves towards the Great Hall. Miss Crawley feeds her lap dog as she walks.

MISS CRAWLEY

Good. Come along, my dear, and sit by me. Then after dinner we shall abuse the company.

Across the room, Lady Southdown speaks to her daughter.

LADY SOUTHDOWN
Really, what hoops she makes us jump through.

LADY JANE
I don't mind, Mama. I like Miss Sharp.

LADY SOUTHDOWN
Caesar liked Brutus and look where it got him.

Sir Pitt gives his arm gruffly to her and Pitt offers his to Jane. Becky goes out with Miss Crawley but she allows herself a quick, careful smile at Rawdon. He smiles back.

INT. GREAT HALL. QUEEN'S CRAWLEY. LATE DAY.
As we know, every effort has been made.

PITT
For what we—

WELLINGTON AND NELSON

THE DUKE OF WELLINGTON (1769-1852) defeated Napoleon's army in the Peninsular War and at Waterloo and was in government service after his career in the military ended. He was Prime Minister from 1828 to 1830 where he opposed parliamentary reform. Despite his splendid military career, his obstinate political views made him unpopular and, on more than one occasion, his house was stoned by angry mobs of people.

ADMIRAL NELSON (1758-1805) lost his right eye in action off Corsica in 1794 and his right arm at Santa Cruz later that year. In 1803 he was given command of the Mediterranean fleet. Despite his wife and the ensuing scandal, for decades he carried on an affair with Emma, Lady Hamilton who was also married. During the Battle of Trafalgar, eighteen out of thirty-three enemy ships were taken or destroyed but Nelson's fleet remained intact. Nelson, himself, was mortally wounded in the battle by a sniper's bullet aboard his flagship, *Victory*.

SIR PITT
Pitt!

Pitt is checked. The company sit and Pitt makes an effort to be agreeable to their honoured guest.

PITT
Aunt Matilda, you are Guest of Honour. What shall we drink to?

She is not to be had by his clumsy blandishments.

MISS CRAWLEY
Better food and a warmer room.

LADY JANE
Should we not drink to peace at last? With Napoleon safe on Elba?

RAWDON
Let's drink to the men who put him there! Wellington and Nelson!

The others raise their glasses but Lady Southdown frowns.

LADY SOUTHDOWN
Wellington I grant you but it is hard to match Nelson's heroism with his private life.

BECKY
Neither Caesar nor Alexander lived lives that bear inspection. Are they not heroes either?

MISS CRAWLEY
Quite right, Miss Sharp, and to me, that was the best part of Nelson's character! He went to the deuce for a woman. There must be good in a man who'll do that. I adore imprudent matches!

Miss Crawley enjoys the freedom that money confers.

LADY SOUTHDOWN
You set no store by birth, then?

MISS CRAWLEY
Birth? Pshaw! Look at this family. We've been at Queen's Crawley since Henry II but is one of us as clever as Miss Sharp?

Lady Southdown opens her mouth to argue but Sir Pitt jumps into the moment to stop her. He raises his glass.

SIR PITT
To all the King's officers!

The others again drink. Lady Southdown is silenced. The footman holds the plate to Miss Crawley's left.

MISS CRAWLEY
Ah. Lobster.

Is she pleased? Nervous glances are exchanged. Then . . .

MISS CRAWLEY
Delicious.

The company breathes again.

INT. MISS CRAWLEY'S BEDROOM. QUEEN'S CRAWLEY. DUSK.
Miss Crawley sits at her dressing table, attended by her maid, Firkin. Becky has come up with her and lingers.

MISS CRAWLEY
Come in, my dear. I've left my toadies in London and what bores they are downstairs. It falls to you to make me laugh. You're clever enough. Isn't she, Firkin?

FIRKIN
I think Miss seems very clever.

Becky and the maid are already enemies.

MISS CRAWLEY
Oh yes, if merit had its reward, you ought to be a duchess.

BECKY
You set no store by birth, then?

A perfect imitation of Lady Southdown. Miss Crawley laughs.

MISS CRAWLEY
Silly old fool, grabbing at my money for that hypocrite Pitt. He should put down his Bible and do the dirty work himself.

BECKY
It is not money but the love of money that's at the root of evil.

This time a perfect Pitt. Miss Crawley peals with laughter.

MISS CRAWLEY
Oh my dear girl, with a decent position, you could put the world on a leash.

BECKY
Perhaps I'll surprise you and run away with a great man.

MISS CRAWLEY
That'd be perfect! I love elopements! I've set my heart on Rawdon running away with someone.

BECKY
A rich someone or a poor someone?

MISS CRAWLEY
Well above all, a *clever* someone. He's the dearest creature but he does need protecting and . . . Oooh.

BECKY
What's the matter?

Miss Crawley clutches her stomach in agony.

MISS CRAWLEY
The lobster. They've poisoned me with that lobster!

INT. GREAT HALL. DUSK.
Rawdon and his father play cards while Pitt walks about with a Bible. There is a cough. Lady Southdown is there.

LADY SOUTHDOWN
I always travel with my medicine chest. Can I not be of any assistance?

Like many wealthy people, it was Miss Crawley's habit to accept as much service as she could get from her inferiors; and good-naturedly to take leave of them when she no longer found them useful. Gratitude among certain rich folks is scarcely natural or to be thought of. They take needy people's services as their due.

—William Makepeace Thackeray, *Vanity Fair*, 1847

PITT

I don't think so, thank you. The doctor is with her now. The best we can do is pray for her soul.

RAWDON (*under his breath*)

And for her hundred thousand.

Rawdon plays his card as a doctor enters.

PITT

Will she live, doctor?

DOCTOR

I've pumped and purged her and I can do no more. It's in the hands of the Lord. You'll settle with me now, Sir Pitt?

SIR PITT

Tomorrow, doctor, if ye don't mind. I only pays by results.

Rawdon and Pitt exchange a glance.

INT. MISS CRAWLEY'S BEDROOM. QUEEN'S CRAWLEY. DAY.

Miss Crawley enjoys playing the invalid. Becky is with her.

MISS CRAWLEY

How do I look?

BECKY

A good deal stronger. They *will* be disappointed.

They both laugh.

BECKY

Lady Southdown hovers at the door night and noon. "I always travel with my medicine chest. Can I not be of any assistance?"

As they laugh together, they are made aware of a figure in the doorway. It is Jane. She smiles gently.

JANE

My mother wondered if you would like a tonic but I see the offer has already been made.

As the door closes, they cannot resist a fit of giggles.

MISS CRAWLEY

That's a dose I doubt I'd live through.

BECKY

Nonsense! It's Captain Rawdon who needs you dead. Lady Southdown and Mr Crawley want you well enough to change your will!

This sets the spoiled spinster off in peals.

MISS CRAWLEY

Rebecca Sharp, I've made up my mind. You must come with me to London. I insist upon it. And so does Byron. We won't be gainsaid, will we?

She appeals to the indifferent mutt.

BECKY

But what could I say to dear Sir Pitt after all his kindness?

It's clear she means to take advantage of the offer.

MISS CRAWLEY

Leave that to me. When a man has two sons and a rich spinster sister, he seldom gainsays her, my dear.

EXT QUEEN'S CRAWLEY, DAY

Rawdon hands them into the coach. Firkin, seething at this special treatment, climbs up. The rest are saying goodbye.

PITT

Must you go, Rawdon? I thought you would stay for some shooting.

Rawdon catches Becky's eye and smiles which Pitt notices.

RAWDON

I'd better see them safe back to Mayfair.

He climbs in and the coach moves off. Sir Pitt sighs sadly.

SIR PITT

There she goes. The best little governess the girls ever had. I suppose I'd better write to Miss Pinkerton for a replacement.

LADY SOUTHDOWN

Let me, Sir Pitt. Miss Pinkerton is an old friend and I should so like to be useful.

And she smiles a secret smile.

INT. COACH. DAY.

They ride along under the gaze of Miss Crawley.

RAWDON

The governor will miss you.

BECKY

Sir Pitt has been good to me.

RAWDON

Who wouldn't be?

Miss Crawley looks over and Rawdon is silent. She hasn't really heard anything. On the seat opposite Becky's hand rests. Gradually, Rawdon's fingers inch across the upholstery and touch hers.

LADY SOUTHDOWN (V.O.)

My dear Miss Pinkerton, a pupil of yours has recently come to my notice. I should so like to know more of her history . . .

His tight boot touches the side of her tiny shoe.

LADY SOUTHDOWN (V.O.)

Her name is Rebecca Sharp . . .

Rawdon stares out of the window. He leans in behind Becky.

RAWDON

Welcome to London.

A nobleman's carriage sweeps by and stops at a great palace that forms the end of the street.

BECKY

Who is that?

MISS CRAWLEY

My neighbour, the Marquess of Steyne. Why?

BECKY

No reason . . .

But there is a reason. She knows that face so well. As Becky leaves the carriage, for a moment, the great man glances back before he enters the doors of Gaunt House.

INT. DRAWING ROOM. OSBORNE HOUSE. EVE.

Mr Osborne is reading the newspaper. His children, George and Maria, who is embroidering, are with him. A loud clock on the mantleshelf ticks the time slowly away. He looks up.

OSBORNE

Going out?

GEORGE

I'm meeting Tarquin and Villiers. And the rest of the chaps. We might play some billiards.

OSBORNE

Ah yes. Lord Tarquin and the Honourable John Villiers.

He rolls the names and titles around his mouth like sweets.

GEORGE

It is not done to pronounce "the Honourable" aloud.

OSBORNE

Well, well. You know these things better than I. What I wonder is: Do they ask you to their homes, these "chaps"? Do you meet their mothers and their sisters?

GEORGE

Sometimes.

OSBORNE

Because you shall not want, you know. The British merchant's son shan't want. You may marry whom you please and keep her well.

MARIA

Father, George is engaged. It's understood—

OSBORNE

Then it can be un-understood! Don't you see, boy? There's nothing you can't have if you will reach for it! Why not a viscount's daughter? Or better yet, an earl's? Or marry an heiress and buy a peerage for yourself!

George and Maria exchange glances.

EXT. ROTTEN ROW. HYDE PARK. DAY.

Miss Crawley and Becky ride in an open *landau* with Rawdon accompanying them on horseback. Becky is reading a letter.

MISS CRAWLEY

You shouldn't read in a carriage. It will make you sick.

RAWDON

Reading always makes me sick.

MISS CRAWLEY

Who is it from?

BECKY

My friend, Amelia Sedley.

MISS CRAWLEY

And what does she say?

BECKY

Nothing much. I thought she might have set a date for her marriage but it seems not.

MISS CRAWLEY

Who is her intended?

BECKY

Captain George Osborne.

MISS CRAWLEY

Any relation to the Duke of Leeds?

BECKY

Oh no, ma'am. He's a tradesman's son.

She is very cool. She knows the rules by now.

RAWDON

I know Osborne. In one of the line regiments. He's as green as this grass and he'll go to the deuce to be seen with a lord. *He pays for their dinner and they take a fortune off him at cards.*

BECKY

Captain Osborne's vanity must make him a tempting victim.

She catches Rawdon's eye. He thinks for a moment.

RAWDON

I say, Aunt. Shall we do Miss Sharp a favour and ask them over?

MISS CRAWLEY

If you think it will be amusing.

She smiles indulgently at Rawdon who shares this generous observation with Becky.

INT. DRAWING ROOM. CRAWLEY HOUSE. EVE.

The five are entering the room. Amelia is with Becky.

AMELIA

I'm glad to see Miss Crawley knows your worth.

BECKY

As long as George knows yours.

AMELIA

Of course he does.

Becky's comment is half serious. Amelia takes it as banter.

BECKY

Shall I play for you?

MISS CRAWLEY

Thank you, my dear. Rawdon, will you explain to Miss Sedley the rules of *piquet*. I have quite forgotten.

BECKY

Be careful, Amelia. Captain Crawley knows his cards.

AMELIA

I'm warned.

RAWDON

There are no fortunes in *piquet*.

BECKY

All the same, be kind to her. She is my only friend.

RAWDON

Not your *only* friend, Miss Sharp.

Becky is playing by now. George joins her.

GEORGE

So, Miss Sharp, how do you like your new place?

BECKY

My place? How kind of you to remind me. It is quite tolerable, thank you, and they treat me very well. But then this is a gentleman's family and quite a change from tradespeople.

She smiles pleasantly as she insults him.

GEORGE

You seemed to like tradespeople well enough last year.

BECKY

Joseph Sedley, you mean? It's true. If he'd asked me I would not have said no.

GEORGE

How very obliging of you.

BECKY

I know what you're thinking. What an honour to have had you for a brother-in-law. Captain George Osborne, son of John Osborne Esquire, son of—what was your grandfather? Never mind. You cannot help your pedigree.

MISS CRAWLEY

Miss Sharp! Come and take over from Rawdon. He is worse than useless!

RAWDON

I admit it. This is not my game. Care for something more grown up, Osborne?

George nods. He has still not recovered from being routed.

INT. ANTE ROOM. CRAWLEY HOUSE. EVE.
The two men are playing.

RAWDON
Monstrous nice gel, Miss Sedley. Lots of tin, I suppose?

GEORGE
How do you find her friend, Miss Sharp?

RAWDON
How do you find her?

GEORGE
Sharp by name and sharp by nature.

Rawdon does not answer but increases his stake.

When attacked sometimes, Becky had a knack of adopting a demure ingénue air, under which she was most dangerous. She said the wickedest things with the most simple unaffected air when in this mood, and would take care artlessly to apologize for her blunders, so that all the world should know that she had made them. —William Makepeace Thackeray, *Vanity Fair*, 1847

GEORGE
I know women. It's well to be on the look out with some of them.

RAWDON
Thank you, old chap.

George matches the stake. Rawdon turns over a Royal Flush.

RAWDON
You're wide awake, I see.

He scoops the money from the table.

EXT. CRAWLEY HOUSE. DUSK.
Amelia's carriage leaves. George rides alongside. Rawdon turns to Becky showing her the roll of notes he has taken.

RAWDON

Cross with me?

BECKY

Cross? I could kiss you! To see George Osborne fleeced makes a perfect end to a perfect day.

RAWDON

Dear me. I rather hoped the evening wasn't over yet . . .

BECKY

Oh?

He hesitates, almost blushing if Rawdon can blush.

RAWDON

I was just wondering if you might like to show me your room . . .

BECKY

Of course.

Rawdon may be surprised but he is delighted until—

BECKY

I'll run and ask Miss Crawley's permission.

RAWDON

Don't joke.

Becky seats herself on a bench in the street. She is enjoying herself.

BECKY

Really, Captain, you cannot imagine I would do anything to incur your aunt's displeasure.

RAWDON

I thought you and I had an understanding.

BECKY

Well, I understand this. Two men and two men only will enter my bedchamber. My husband and the doctor.

Rawdon is not insulted but they have to face facts.

RAWDON

You know my heart, Becky. You know I'd do anything for you.

BECKY

I'm flattered.

RAWDON

But Aunt Tilly's views on these things came out of the Ark.

BECKY

That's not how she sounds.

RAWDON

Don't be deceived. She talks like Cromwell but she thinks like Charles the First and it's an outside wager she'll ever change her mind.

There is a moment of silence between them. Then:

BECKY

Then it's lucky, Captain, you're a gambling man and no stranger to taking a chance . . .

And away she goes back through the open front door.

INT. DRAWING ROOM. SEDLEY HOUSE. DAY.

Amelia is writing a letter. Her mother is once more sewing.

AMELIA (V.O.)

Dearest Becky, a letter from Jos arrived from India this morning, filled with regrets about a certain person. I should tell him, dear Becky, he has missed his chance, for his goddess has acquired other suitors. Your loving friend, Amelia Sedley.

MRS SEDLEY

Has Miss Sharp taken to Mayfair?

AMELIA

She seems quite at home in her new life.

MRS SEDLEY

I do not doubt it. I had thought her a mere social climber. I see now she's a mountaineer.

INT. MISS CRAWLEY'S BEDROOM. CRAWLEY HOUSE. DAY.

The letter is held open. There is the signature, "your loving friend, Amelia Sedley." Becky folds it away. In a huge, linen-draped tub next to the fire, Miss Crawley is being bathed by Firkin while Becky sorts through the post.

BECKY

This one's for you. It's from Mr Pitt.

MISS CRAWLEY

Read it.

BECKY

"Dear Aunt, I have both happy and sad news to relay. The good news is that I am married. Lady Jane Sheepshanks has done me the honour of becoming my wife."

MISS CRAWLEY

No great surprise there. She's a nice enough girl although I do not envy him his mother-in-law. What is the bad news?

BECKY

"I am sorry to tell you that my step-mother, Lady Crawley, has gone to a better place."

MISS CRAWLEY

That's not very helpful. After Queen's Crawley, almost anywhere's a better place.

BECKY

Poor lady. She had a good heart.

MISS CRAWLEY

Nonsense. She sold her heart long ago to become a baronet's wife. But then what else would you expect from an ironmonger's daughter? What's that?

There's a noise in the street and a bell rings. Becky goes to the window.

EXT. CURZON STREET. DAY.

Sir Pitt is standing on the front step.

BECKY (V.O.)

Good gracious! Here's Sir Pitt!

INT. MISS CRAWLEY'S BEDROOM. CRAWLEY HOUSE. DAY.

MISS CRAWLEY

My dear, I cannot see him. My nerves are really not up to it.

INT. DRAWING ROOM. CRAWLEY HOUSE. DAY.

Sir Pitt enters with Becky. He shuts the door.

SIR PITT

It's not Miss Crawley I want to see. It's you. You have to come back to Queen's Crawley. You've heard my news?

BECKY

Only just now. I'm very sorry and if there's anything I can do—

SIR PITT

There is! There's plenty for you to do! Everything's wrong since you left! You must come back!

To her astonishment, he kneels before her.

SIR PITT (cont'd)

Marry me. Come as Lady Crawley, if you like, but do come back.

INT. LANDING. CRAWLEY HOUSE. DAY.

Firkin is at the keyhole. At this last exchange, she jerks back and gallops up the stairs two at a time.

INT. MISS CRAWLEY'S BEDROOM. CRAWLEY HOUSE. DAY.

Firkin stands at the door. She has delivered her news.

MISS CRAWLEY

What!

Miss Crawley bounces out of the bath like a girl.

INT DRAWING ROOM.

SIR PITT

Don't keep me down here forever.

BECKY

Oh, Sir Pitt, I can't!

Miss Crawley enters in a *peignoir*, as tense as a wire.

SIR PITT

Can't or won't? Would you not like to be an old man's darling?

BECKY

No, Sir Pitt, I *really* can't. The truth is I am married already.

SIR PITT

Oh well, it was worth a try.

As he gets to his feet Miss Crawley relaxes.

MISS CRAWLEY

Married! Well, what a chance is lost! Never mind, my dear, we'll set him up, won't we, brother? I'll buy him a shop or commission a portrait. Whoever he is, he and his family are lucky to have you.

BECKY

I hope you think so.

MISS CRAWLEY

Indeed I do.

Emboldened, Becky takes both their hands.

BECKY

Then if you cannot take me for a wife and sister . . . Will you not love me as daughter and niece?

SIR PITT

Wha—

BECKY

Dear Sir Pitt, dearest Miss Crawley, it's true. I have married Rawdon.

Sir Pitt Crawley is quite disgusting really. He's landed gentry. He has plenty of land but the whole family is falling apart; his wife is barmy and they don't have any money. Actually, he's not a bad old stick and I quite like him. I think he's the only one in the story who really understands Becky and admires her for what she is. He proposes to her but, of course, she has bigger fish to fry. —Bob Hoskins

SIR PITT

Rawdon!

MISS CRAWLEY

MY Rawdon!!!

With a scream of horror, Miss Crawley faints dead away.

EXT. CRAWLEY HOUSE. DUSK.
Becky comes out. Behind her Firkin carries her trunk.

BECKY

Look after her, Firkin ... Poor dear Miss Crawley. I do worry so.

FIRKIN

Don't waste your syrup on me, Miss Sharp. Just get back in the knife-box where you belong.

She throws the trunk into the street and slams the door. This is witnessed by the driver of a passing coal cart.

DRIVER

Are you all right, Miss?

BECKY

I will be if you're going past Baker Street.

DRIVER

But would that be proper, Miss?

He may be shocked but she isn't. Becky Sharp is no snob.

BECKY

More proper than standing here on the street. Give us a hand with the trunk.

At a window in Gaunt House, Lord Steyne stands, watching. As the cart moves off, she catches Steyne's eye and smiles. The great nobleman allows himself to smile back.

EXT. A RUN DOWN STREET IN LONDON. NIGHT.
This is a slightly seedy part of town. A card in the windows of some of them announce rooms to let.

INT. RAWDON'S LODGINGS. NIGHT.
In a plain room, Becky and Rawdon are in bed together.

RAWDON

We'll be in Queer Street if she *don't* come round.

BECKY

Better Queer Street with you than Park Lane with any other. But Rawdon, she will come round. She said herself she'd love you to elope.

RAWDON

It's all talk. She likes romance in her novels but not in her family. Where they're concerned she's as snobbish as Queen Charlotte.

BECKY

Then we must send an ambassador to plead our case.

RAWDON

What sort of ambassador?

BECKY

I'd say a very little one with rosy cheeks and blue eyes and probably not too much hair ...

For a moment Rawdon is puzzled. Then:

RAWDON

What? You mean ... ? Oh my darling, brilliant girl! Well that'll mend our fences if nothing else will!

And he starts to make love to his wife.

EXT. OSBORNE HOUSE. DAY.
Osborne is near his door when Sedley steps out of the shadows where he has been concealed. He starts to argue and gesticulate but Osborne brushes him off and goes inside.

OSBORNE

What do you want?

SEDLEY

Time, Osborne, that's what I want.

OSBORNE

I owe you nothing! I will give you nothing!

SEDLEY

You owe me friendship.

OSBORNE

You have no friendship coming from me.

Osborne shuts the door on him.

INT. MISS CRAWLEY'S BEDROOM. CRAWLEY HOUSE. DAY.

Miss Crawley is receiving a manicure and a pedicure from Firkin. This time Lady Southdown is the witness.

LADY SOUTHDOWN

When one thinks of how she tended you! And all the time . . .

MISS CRAWLEY

I should have guessed that nobody does anything for nothing. But for a pauper's daughter, a penniless governess, to make off with my Rawdon!

She snuffles a bit. In truth, she is calming down.

MISS CRAWLEY

At least her mother was a Montmorency. I suppose we must cling to that.

Lady Southdown strikes.

LADY SOUTHDOWN

Not a bit of it! I have it on the best authority: Her mother was an opera-girl in the chorus at Montmartre!

Miss Crawley falls back with a little scream. She nods.

MISS CRAWLEY

Very well. I know what I must do. Would you be good enough to bring my little desk here?

Lady Southdown bounds eagerly to fetch the writing box.

MISS CRAWLEY

I am almost sorry for poor Rawdon but I cannot let her profit from her scheming.

LADY SOUTHDOWN

Nor should you! I'm glad to see you've changed your opinions. You remember when you told us all at Queen's Crawley that you adored imprudent marriages.

Miss Crawley sinks into her pillows.

MISS CRAWLEY

Not *in real life!*

INT. DINING ROOM. SEDLEY HOUSE. DAY.

Mr Sedley and Amelia are breakfasting with Mrs Sedley who reads a newspaper as she prattles on. He is silent.

MRS SEDLEY

We only have forty of the silver-handled knives so I've asked Mr Renwick to look out for any of a similar pattern . . . Oh, listen to this: Emperor Napoleon Escapes from Elba and Marches on Paris. Allies Prepare for War. Amelia? What's the matter, dear?

Amelia's face is as white as snow.

AMELIA

Will . . . will it affect George?

MRS SEDLEY

He's a soldier, isn't he, for all his swagger and there's more to soldiering than gold braid and regimental dinners. Now, have we enough of the blue-edged plates? It's to be a buffet and I don't want to risk the Crown Derby—

With a smothered cry, Amelia runs from the room.

MRS SEDLEY

Amelia! Tsk. If she means to be a soldier's wife she must learn to bear such things . . . I've been thinking about the fruit we need—

She is silenced by Sedley's harsh voice.

SEDLEY

She'll have a great deal more to bear before the day is through.

He slumps back. His eyes are filled with tears.

SEDLEY

I must tell you. I can put it off no longer . . . We're ruined, Mary. Lost. Everything is gone. We must begin again.

The poor woman cannot take it in.

MRS SEDLEY

But . . . we're giving a soiree . . .

SEDLEY

There'll be no more soirees or balls or dinners either. That life is finished for us.

MRS SEDLEY
But . . . can it be as bad as that?

SEDLEY

It's worse. And that's not all. The debt that finished me, the man who tipped me into the abyss, that man is none other than John Osborne.

MRS SEDLEY
My God, my God, this will break her heart!

INT. DINING ROOM. SEDLEY HOUSE. DAY.

A gavel smashes down. It is the same room but much changed. Rows of chairs face an auctioneer.

AUCTIONEER

By order of the trustees of the Sedley Estate, this auction will now commence. Lot 368, an inlaid ebony writing desk. Shall we say four guineas? 5? Anymore? Come on . . . going, going SOLD! Lot 369. A modern, upright piano. We will start at three guineas.

BECKY

I sang to that.

She is standing at the back with Rawdon.

RAWDON

Would you like it?

He puts his hand up.

AUCTIONEER

Five at the back. Six.

Becky looks over to who is bidding against them.

BECKY

It's Captain Dobbin.

RAWDON

I know him. He's in the Ninth.

BECKY

Let him have it. Don't bid again.

AUCTIONEER

Sold. To the Captain. Lot 370. A landscape signed Francis Sharp 1801. Shall we say five guineas?

Becky gasps.

RAWDON

What's the matter?

BECKY

My father painted it. I gave it to Amelia.

RAWDON

I'll get it for you.

He makes a sign and the auctioneer takes his bid but then:

AUCTIONEER

Six at the back.

The bidding climbs on up until . . .

RAWDON

Nineteen.

AUCTIONEER

Twenty at the back.

Becky lays her hand on Rawdon's arm.

BECKY

Leave it. It doesn't matter.

Rawdon shakes his head at the auctioneer.

AUCTIONEER

Sold! For twenty guineas to the Marquess of Steyne.

Becky turns to look at that cold, proud profile. Feeling her gaze upon him, he turns. Rawdon is puzzled.

RAWDON

Why would Lord Steyne bother with a little auction like this?

BECKY

He collects my father's works. A true collector will go anywhere to get what he wants.

They make their way to the door. Dobbin is also leaving.

BECKY

Captain Dobbin.

DOBBIN

Miss Sharp—I beg your pardon, Mrs Crawley. Crawley.

BECKY

Are you taking up the piano, Captain?

DOBBIN

I have a friend who will get some use from it, I think.

BECKY

Indeed she will.

She is gently amused by Dobbin's fidelity.

EXT. SEDLEY COTTAGE. FULHAM. DAY.

Dobbin approaches the modest front door.

INT. PARLOUR. SEDLEY COTTAGE. FULHAM. DAY.

Dobbin is with Mrs Sedley and Amelia, lethargic with grief.

DOBBIN

I saw Miss Sharp at the auction. At least—I should say Mrs Crawley now.

AMELIA

But how is George? Have you any news?

MRS SEDLEY

That's right. Let's talk of George Osborne when all the world is falling about our ears.

AMELIA

Mama . . .

DOBBIN

George is well, I think. But busy.

MRS SEDLEY

Too busy to come here. I'll fetch some tea.

She goes out, furious at the desertion of her vain godson.

AMELIA

Mama does not understand the calls that are made upon his time . . .

But her face is grey with misery as she goes to fetch an envelope. Inside is a miniature of herself.

AMELIA

When next you see him, would you give him this? I painted it. It's not wrong is it, to remind him of the one who loves him most?

DOBBIN

Of course not. But why not wait and give it him yourself?

AMELIA

He never visits now. I would have sent it but I sometimes wonder if he gets my letters . . .

Old Sedley wanders in. His eyes are somehow changed.

SEDLEY

Mrs Sedley says you've been to the auction, Captain. My office juniors went yesterday. They sent us round these spoons.

He shows a package holding some silver teaspoons.

DOBBIN

That was kind of them.

SEDLEY

Yes. It was, wasn't it? After a lifetime of labour, it's good to have some spoons to show for it.

He covers his face with his hand and starts to cry. Amelia goes to him but he shakes her off and goes out.

DOBBIN

Mr Sedley does not seem quite himself.

AMELIA

We are none of us ourselves, Captain. Not any more.

Dobbin opens his mouth to answer but Amelia's attention has gone to the window. Suddenly her face lights up like the sun coming out from a cloud. With a cry, she runs out.

EXT. SEDLEY COTTAGE. FULHAM. DAY.

A cart with the recently purchased piano is by the kerb. The men are lifting it down as Amelia runs forward and almost literally caresses the instrument. Dobbin comes out.

AMELIA

Look! Look what he's done! Isn't it wonderful!

For a second, he might claim her gratitude but looking at her transformed face, he cannot bring himself to spoil it.

DOBBIN

Wonderful.

AMELIA

I can't believe it! Oh thank God, *thank God! Mama!* It's all right! George has bought the piano for me and he'll be here directly!

She is running back inside when she stops, turning back.

AMELIA

He will be here directly, won't he?

The desperate need in her eyes is too much to resist.

DOBBIN

I'd stake my life on it.

INT. HALL AND STAIRCASE. OSBORNE HOUSE. DAY.
George is fencing with Dobbin in a light-hearted way.

GEORGE

Don't nag. You know the Guv'nor wasn't keen on the match before. You can guess what he thinks of it now.

DOBBIN

Because she's lost her "money" and "position"?

GEORGE

You needn't say them as if they tasted nasty. Dash it, Figs, I'm fond of Amelia and all that, but Sedley's gone belly up and it's changed things, whether you like it or not.

He breaks off to find a cigar in a case in his coat and looks about for a light. Dobbin also picks up his coat and sees the envelope Amelia gave him in his pocket.

DOBBIN

Oh. Miss Sedley asked me to give you this when I next saw you.

George nods, takes it and holds it in the fire as a spill.

DOBBIN

George, for God's sake! You haven't opened it!

GEORGE

No need. They're all the same.

Just then the door opens. Osborne Senior appears.

OSBORNE

George? What are you playing at? We're waiting for you.

He snatches up George's coat and helps him into it then, through the dialogue, buttons him into it like a child. George looks across at Dobbin with a half shrug.

GEORGE

There's some friend of Maria's they want me to meet.

Osborne also looks fiercely at the newcomer.

DOBBIN

I'm just leaving, Sir.

Osborne barely acknowledges this but goes to the door to wait for his son. As George passes him, Dobbin whispers.

DOBBIN

I tell you, George, you must go to her. She's dying.

In the flames Amelia's picture curls and burns.

INT. DRAWING ROOM. OSBORNE HOUSE. DAY.
George enters with his father to find Maria with Miss Rhoda Swartz, an intelligent-looking young woman of mixed blood.

OSBORNE

May I present my son, George? This is Miss Rhoda Swartz. Miss Rhoda was talking of Jamaica and her sugar plantations there.

RHODA

Though I don't remember it. I left when I was three.

Mira is a horse whisperer. She lets you be and then she sidles up after a take and gives you practical factory-floor notes that improve your performance, as opposed to some kind of affable psychological mish-mash you can't use. She's very practical and it's just great watching her work with every actor – from the extras to Reese Witherspoon, everyone gets the same attention and everyone's appreciated equally. —Rhys Ifans

Osborne gives a mixture between a cough and a chuckle.

OSBORNE
Maria, may I borrow you for a moment? Can you forgive us?

George and Rhoda are left alone. Rhoda breaks the silence.

RHODA
Your father does not much trouble to conceal his plans.

GEORGE
Which are?

RHODA
For us to marry, of course.

GEORGE
Indeed?

RHODA
Come. Sit by me.

George crosses the room to sit by Rhoda.

RHODA
Let us speak frankly. My fortune is great, my birth is not. So I must choose between a poor nobleman or a rich *bourgeois* like you.

GEORGE
'Pon my word, you've a very precise grasp of the matter.

RHODA
I would have liked a title but my guardian says if you and I combine our fortunes, we may buy one whenever we wish.

GEORGE
Astute, your guardian . . . Will you excuse me?

He bows stiffly and starts towards the door.

INT. DINING ROOM. OSBORNE HOUSE. DAY.
Osborne is reading by the fire. George enters in a rage.

GEORGE
I cannot *believe* you are seriously suggesting Miss Swartz as the companion of my heart and hearth!

OSBORNE
Why not?

GEORGE
Well, to start with . . . she is not English.

OSBORNE
Hoity toity! Less fastidious if you please! What's a shade or so of tawny with half a million on the table? Why, with that money we'll have you in the House of Lords in no time! Just think! Dining at Kew, dancing at Carlton House—

GEORGE
And what of honour, sir?

OSBORNE
Honour?

GEORGE
Yes, honour. You may buy a string of ancestors to hang upon your walls but I see you have not bought the breeding that goes with them! You made me give my word to Amelia—

George has used the best weapon he can think of to spoil his father's fantasies and Osborne is scared of his son.

OSBORNE
Be silent, Sir! Do you dare to speak that object's name to me!

GEORGE
Dare, Sir, is not a word to be used to a Captain in the British army. For I *am* a gentleman though I am your son! I beg you to use language I'm accustomed to.

OSBORNE
Pshaw! I shall say what I like to my own child! And I say this: I have not slaved for forty years to see you marry a beggar maid!

GEORGE
You made the match!

OSBORNE
And I can *un*make it! You will marry whom I say, Sir! And I say you will marry Miss Swartz! Either that or you take your pack and walk out of this house without a shilling! Do I make myself clear, Sir?

GEORGE
As a bell, Sir.

And he slams the door behind him.

EXT. OSBORNE HOUSE. DAY.

A boisterous group of men carrying the Union Jack congregate on the street corner, recruiting soldiers for the imminent war. A coach pulls to a halt and a man steps forward. It is Dobbin. Osborne gets out. He holds up his hand.

OSBORNE

If you're here to plead his case, you have made a wasted journey.

DOBBIN

Mr Osborne, we're on the brink of war. Should anything happen to George you wouldn't forgive yourself if you had not parted in charity. May I not take him a message from you? Please.

This speech brings Osborne to a halt. His shoulders sag. The old curmudgeon longs for his son. He sighs. He turns.

OSBORNE

Very well. Let him come back. Tell him if Miss Swartz does not please him, we'll find another who will. Let him only come home to his old room and things will be as they were before.

DOBBIN

They cannot be.

OSBORNE

Why not? If I say they can?

DOBBIN

Because George married Miss Sedley this morning. I go from here to their wedding breakfast. Will you not come with me?

This speech has the opposite of the desired effect.

Old Osborne stood in secret terror of his son as a better gentleman than himself; and perhaps my readers may have remarked in their experience of this Vanity Fair of ours, that there is no character which a low-minded man so much mistrusts as that of a gentleman.

—William Makepeace Thackeray, *Vanity Fair*, 1847

OSBORNE

Now I see how it is! It is you, Captain! You who have urged my own boy to defy me! You who has pushed a beggar into my family! Curse you, Sir! Out of my way!

Osborne turns away with a muttered oath and strides into the house. The door slams shut in Dobbin's face.

INT. DRAWING ROOM. OSBORNE HOUSE. NIGHT.

Mr Osborne has the family Bible open. Weeping silently, he picks up a pen and carefully strikes out George's name.

INT/EXT. THE ORANGERY OF A LONDON HOTEL. DAY.

A punch bowl, ladled out amid much merriment, tells us the Crawleys and Jos Sedley have gathered to celebrate the marriage. Behind them a table is set for a feast. Dobbin arrives and George hurries to greet him.

GEORGE

Well?

DOBBIN

He would not come.

GEORGE

And he sent no message?

DOBBIN

None that you would care to hear.

GEORGE

What a fool I am! One sordid little ceremony, half an hour of my life, and I'm a beggar. And all because of a fit of pique!

Joseph Sedley is with Amelia. She is charming in her wedding finery, with orange blossom in her hair.

AMELIA

Mama and Papa are so anxious to see you while you are here. Jos, will you not do something to help them? They are your parents.

JOSEPH

Believe me, I would but my expenses in India overwhelm me . . .

Becky is with Rawdon. They are looking across at George.

RAWDON

He has a sense of honour then.

BECKY

Well, someone does . . .

She indicates Dobbin.

RAWDON

You think the Best Man had a part in it?

BECKY

I do. And this time the best man didn't win.

On the other side of the chamber, George is still seething.

Amelia comes up.

AMELIA

IS everything all right, George?

GEORGE

I was just thinking. There is much to be said for marriage. When the couple is well suited.

He is watching Becky sparkling at Rawdon's side. Amelia takes this as a compliment but Dobbin, following his gaze, knows better. Rawdon and Becky are talking to Sedley.

BECKY

So, have you found many changes since your last visit from India?

JOSEPH

Some. And one in particular that I very much regret.

He gives her a meaningful look. Becky taps his arm with her fan. She bears him no grudge and they are friends again. The manager of the hotel approaches Rawdon.

RAWDON

Is it time to sit down?

MANAGER

Whenever you wish, Captain, but a message has arrived and the boy is waiting for an answer.

Rawdon opens the envelope. He looks around the room.

RAWDON

Dobbin! Osborne! There's news here for all of us. It's the order for Belgium. We embark next week.

As he gives the answer to the manager and steers the company towards the table, Amelia has turned pale as death.

She might faint but George catches her sharply by the elbow.

GEORGE

Pull yourself together and come to the table.

BECKY

Men need war like the soil needs turning. Oh I'll enjoy it!

George steers his wife to where Becky is presiding over the high spirited table. Dobbin looks anxiously at Amelia.

JOSEPH

You're not going over there in your condition?

BECKY

Of course I'm going! Why should the men have all the fun? And didn't Eleanor of Aquitaine ride into battle pregnant and bare breasted?

RAWDON

Bravo! And by Gad, if there's a woman alive who could do the same, it's you!

DOBBIN

Be careful of the model, Mrs Crawley. Queen Eleanor was locked up by her husband.

BECKY

And emerged from her prison to govern England!

RAWDON

What about you, Sedley? Will you join the excursion?

SEDLEY

If it weren't for my duties in India, I would be there like a shot.

From the general laugh, it's clear no one believes him. Amelia speaks softly into the hilarity.

AMELIA

I will go.

DOBBIN

You cannot! Think of the danger . . .

RAWDON

Why shouldn't she? She can keep Becky company while we men make history!

EXT. PALACE. NIGHT.

A title tells us: **Brussels - 17th June 1815**

Around the square, soldiers loitering in groups or warming their hands on braziers show us that this is now a garrison town. Footmen with flambeaux line the steps leading up to the palace entrance. Carriages disgorge guests aflame with orders and jewels. George is walking with Amelia.

AMELIA

We won't know anyone.

GEORGE

Who's fault is that? If you would only put yourself out to be civil once in a while. The Crawleys have been here no longer than us and Mrs Crawley is the talk of the town.

AMELIA

Is that what you would have me? The "talk of the town"?

GEORGE

You know what I mean. You grumble that you're lonely and now you complain because you're invited to the Duchess of Richmond's ball! If you knew what Mrs Crawley had to go through to arrange it.

AMELIA

I can imagine.

This is not quite as reverential as George would have it.

AMELIA

Don't be cross with me, George. I do so hate it when you are.

He is mollified by her humility but his attention is taken by the arrival below them of the Crawleys' coach.

Rawdon climbs out and holds his hand for Becky. She emerges into the flickering light. She is dazzling.

INT. FOYER OF THE BALLROOM. NIGHT.

As Becky walks towards the ballroom, other guests see her.

BAREACRES

Here comes the famous Mrs Crawley.

LADY BAREACRES

Though why she is famous is a mystery to me! Why does everyone receive her? As for General Tufto!

BAREACRES

He must find her command of French useful.

LORD DARLINGTON

I know I would.

He and Bareacres share their admiration of Becky which annoys their wives.

LADY BAREACRES

A *real* lady would not speak it half as well.

LADY DARLINGTON

Hush, my dear.

Becky and Rawdon have drawn level with them.

BECKY

Lady Bareacres, Lady Darlington.

BAREACRES

Good evening, Mrs Crawley.

He gives a slight bow as she nods and passes on.

LADY BAREACRES

You're making an exhibition of yourself.

INT. BALLROOM. NIGHT.

Once in the ballroom, the measure of Becky's sensational success is clear from the reaction to them. Across the room, George and Amelia stand untalked-to. He spies Becky.

GEORGE

Wait here a minute.

AMELIA

George, I feel a little s—

But he has walked away from his wife without another word.

Across the ballroom, Rawdon touches Becky's arm.

RAWDON

Can I leave you in charge? I see some sheep that need shearing.

He looks at a cardroom where some eager young men play. She responds by nodding towards the advancing General Tufto.

BECKY

Go. You manage our income while I see to your career . . . good evening, General.

TUFTO

Evening, Crawley. Mrs Crawley, lovely as ever. Can I tempt you to a turn about the room?

She takes his arm as George arrives.

GEORGE

Mrs Crawley, I hope your dance card isn't quite filled yet.

BECKY

Hardly. I've just arrived.

GEORGE

I am the early bird, then.

BECKY

And I, presumably, the worm.

Tufto laughs and so does she but she takes pity.

BECKY

General, do you know Captain Osborne of the Ninth? That is Osborne with an "e". Make sure you spell it right when you mention him in dispatches.

TUFTO

If only spelling was my forte.

Amelia watches George flirt with Becky and suck up to the General. Nearby, Lady Darlington is talking to her husband.

LADY DARLINGTON
There she goes, leading the General round like a pig on a string.

LORD DARLINGTON
If you'd helped my career half as much as she's helped Crawley's, I'd be Commander in Chief by now.

LADY DARLINGTON
Then it's as well I haven't. Or Napoleon would be camped in Windsor Castle.

Suddenly, Amelia clasps her hand over her mouth. Looking anx-

iously round, she scurries behind a pillar and finds a welcome potted palm. Bending low, she throws up.

DOBBIN (V.O.)

Would you like me to fetch some water? Or a chair? Or a doctor?

Shutting her eyes with embarrassment, Amelia stands. The panic in Dobbin's eyes is her remedy. She laughs.

AMELIA
Calm yourself, Captain. One look around the ballroom should tell you a great many women have gone through it before me.

Becky, waltzing with George, has been watching.

BECKY

Is Amelia all right?

GEORGE

I expect so. Dobbin's with her.

BECKY

Shouldn't you have more care of her? Now?

GEORGE

You mean now that yet another rope has come to bind me?

She raises her eyebrows.

GEORGE

You are not like Amelia, Mrs Crawley. Nothing will quench your fire. My wife is different . . .

These words are not quite welcome to Becky. The waltz ends.

BECKY

I'm quite tired. Could you fetch me my shawl and my nosegay?

GEORGE

Of course.

He goes off. Becky strolls past where Lady Bareacres, in her diamonds, is with Lady Darlington. Becky smiles.

BECKY

How prettily the Duchess has arranged things.

LADY BAREACRES

She always does . . . Or don't you go to her parties in England?

Becky swallows the insult and moves on.

LADY BAREACRES

No matter. After all, we won't know her back in London.

INT. FOYER OF THE BALLROOM. NIGHT.

Dobbin is with Amelia.

DOBBIN

I wish you would let me come with you.

AMELIA

No. I mean it. Go back at once.

DOBBIN

I'll tell George you're safe.

AMELIA

Don't. It will only annoy him that I've left the ball early.

DOBBIN

But why did he bring you at all?

She shrugs. Her bleakness stabs him through the heart.

DOBBIN

Just tell me you're happy.

AMELIA

Oh yes. *No marriage is a fairy tale, Captain, however one might wish it so.* We're happy enough.

DOBBIN

I should feel very guilty if you were not . . .

AMELIA

Why? It was not of your making.

It was but he cannot tell her. He takes a deep breath.

DOBBIN

We are at war and war makes men brave. Even off the battlefield.

As for [Becky] shining in society, it was no fault of hers; she was formed to shine there. Was there any woman who could talk, or sing, or do anything like her?

—William Makepeace Thackeray, *Vanity Fair*, 1847

She looks at him curiously.

DOBBIN

Mrs Osborne. Amelia. If ever you should need a friend you know that, while there is breath in my body, you have one.

It is as near a declaration of love as he can make.

AMELIA

Dear William, you're kind but don't worry. George and I will do very well.

DOBBIN

And George is happy? About . . . ?

AMELIA

Of course. Yes, he is pleased. I think . . . At least he will be when he gets used to the idea. Now, do go back to the ball. Good night.

She can't see the love or the pain as he watches her go.

INT. BALLROOM. NIGHT.

In the card room, Becky walks towards Rawdon's table. With laughter and the odd groan of despair, beauties and beaux are losing fortunes. A woman rips the diamonds from her throat, casting them onto the table with the recklessness of war. George joins Becky. He gives her the bouquet and shawl with an intent look. A folded note hides among the flowers. She checks to see if Rawdon has noticed but he only winks secretly at her with a nod towards George.

RAWDON

So, Osborne, are you ready for a hand at cards?

GEORGE

If Mrs Crawley . . . ?

BECKY

Of course! Who knows? Tonight I sense you may be lucky!

With such empty promises does she control her admirers. Sliding away, she takes the note and hides it in her bosom. But before George can sit down to play, Dobbin emerges from the crowd and hurries over to him.

GEORGE

Dobbs! Come and have a drink!

DOBBIN

No. Come out, George, don't drink anymore.

GEORGE

Nonsense Dobbo. Have a drink yourself and light up your lantern jaw. Here's to you.

The shouting is growing louder in different parts of the room. Women are crying as men are running out.

GEORGE

What's happening?

Before Dobbin can answer, General Tufto has stepped onto the stage and silenced the band. He speaks loud and clear.

TUFTO

Your Grace, my lords, ladies and gentlemen! The enemy has passed the River Sambre and our left is already engaged. We march in three hours.

As the band starts up with a military air, Becky hurries into Rawdon's embrace. All around them, cards are thrown down, supper rooms empty and the ballroom floor is abandoned as the dancers are transformed into soldiers and tomorrow's widows.

INT. CRAWLEY LODGINGS. BRUSSELS. NIGHT.

Becky is in her nightdress. Her pregnancy is quite obvious. She watches as Rawdon strips off his dress uniform.

RAWDON

I'm not afraid but I'm a big target for a shot and if I should go down, I want you to know what there is for you. I've had a good run here so you've a wad of money. There's a horse left to sell and that dressing case is worth three hundred.

BECKY

You mean we owe three hundred on it.

RAWDON

I'll wear my old uniform, so you can sell the new one. With the saddles, guns, rings and the sable cloak, there's enough to keep you dry and get you to England before . . .

He steps forward to run his hands tenderly over her.

BECKY

I'll manage.

RAWDON

Won't you just! There was never a woman who could manage like you, Becky Sharp.

She responds to his embrace, running her hands over his bare chest. She is perhaps surprised by her own emotions.

BECKY

Oh, Rawdon, *you will be careful?* Don't do anything brave. *You won't, will you? Promise?*

RAWDON

What? Tears? From my strong little Becky?

BECKY

And why not? I'm a woman in love, aren't I? *We're supposed to cry.*

RAWDON

Oh my darling, if you awake to find me dead, you can be sure at least of this. Whatever life may have in store for you, you are a woman who has been truly loved . . .

He kisses her passionately.

INT. OSBORNE LODGINGS. BRUSSELS. NIGHT.
George, still in his dress uniform, is writing.

GEORGE (V.O.)
. . . forgive me if you can and try to remember your loving and grateful son, George."

He seals the letter. There is a voice from the bed.

AMELIA
I'm awake, George. Can I help you to change?

GEORGE
No time. I'll go as I am.

He takes off his ornamental sash and throws it down then moves towards the pitiful figure of his wife.

GEORGE
I've left a letter for my father. See that he gets it if . . .

She flings her arms round his neck.

AMELIA
Of course I will . . . Oh, George. I've disappointed you. I know I have. Can you forgive me?

Looking at her, just this once, he has a decent instinct.

GEORGE

Do not say sorry to me. It is I who am sorry. If I've been cruel—

But her kiss stops his mouth as, outside, the cannons boom.

EXT. BRUSSELS. DAY.

There is universal panic. The citizens run this way and that, dragging children and possessions in their wake.

LADY BAREACRES

Mrs Crawley! Mrs Crawley, over here, if you please!

Lord and Lady Bareacres sit in a two-seater trap with no animal between the shafts. They have spied Becky in the crowd.

BECKY

Lady Bareacres. What a surprise.

LADY BAREACRES

We sent our servant to the inn for a horse but the only one left is Captain Crawley's.

BECKY

Fancy.

LADY BAREACRES

What will you take for it?

BECKY

Nothing from you, my lady. *Not even your wonderful diamonds which I presume are sewn inside your dress.*

LADY BAREACRES

Don't be silly, my dear. We've always been friends, have we not?

BECKY

No. We have not.

LADY BAREACRES

Now listen to me. You may come with us if you wish but we must and we will have that horse!

Becky laughs in her face and moves on as they continue to bleat her name increasingly desperately. Lord Darlington hurries up.

LORD DARLINGTON

Discretion being the better part of valour, Mrs Crawley, I'm afraid it is time to quit Brussels.

BECKY

Are we really losing?

LORD DARLINGTON

They say the enemy has broken through the line . . . Which brings me to the point. Did you sell Lady Bareacres your horse?

BECKY

Doesn't anyone love me for myself alone? No, I didn't.

She thinks. He has, after all, been pleasanter than most.

BECKY

You may buy it if you give me a seat in your carriage.

LORD DARLINGTON

Done.

EXT. BRUSSELS. DAY.

Amelia is in the crowd, half crazy with fear, a latter day Ophelia. She stops a running man.

AMELIA

Please! Help me! What news is there? Do you know what's happened to the Ninth?

But he runs on, leaving her to the buffeting crush.

The Darlingtons are in a small coach with a single horse and only one empty seat. Soldiers, wounded and bleeding, stagger past in the escaping mass.

LADY DARLINGTON

Why must she come with us?

LORD DARLINGTON

First, because I like her, second she's pregnant and third it was the condition that gave us the horse.

Becky, with a packed case, is running through the crowd.

LORD DARLINGTON

Hurry, Mrs Crawley! We must leave now!

She quickens her pace but then she hears Amelia's voice.

AMELIA

Somebody! Anybody! Have you seen Captain Osborne? Captain George Osborne of the Ninth!

BECKY

Amelia! What are you doing? You shouldn't be out here.

LORD DARLINGTON

Mrs Crawley! Come now if you're coming.

She runs back to the coach, dragging Amelia with her.

BECKY

Lord Darlington, is there room for Mrs Osborne?

LADY DARLINGTON

Only if you give up your place.

AMELIA

Don't worry about me. I'll wait here for George, whatever comes.

Becky looks from her friend to the carriage and steps back.

BECKY

We will meet again in London.

LORD DARLINGTON

I hope so! Good luck to you!

The carriage is gone. Amelia blunders on through the crowd.

AMELIA

Surely someone has news of George Osborne? There must be word of my George?

She is almost hysterical. Becky takes hold of her.

BECKY

Amelia, you must take hold of yourself. We are soldiers' wives, we live with uncertainty.

AMELIA

How would you feel if you had spent last night alone while your husband danced with another woman? If you have stolen his last evening from me, I will never forgive you!

BECKY

How could you say such a thing? But if you must hear the truth, your George is not—

AMELIA

My George is not what?

Becky had been going to reveal that George is not what Amelia thinks him but she decides against it.

BECKY

Is not the man to see you risk your health or his baby. Come inside and we'll wait together.

With her arm around her, Becky takes Amelia to her door.

INT. OSBORNE LODGINGS. BRUSSELS. NIGHT.

Amelia lies on the bed, holding George's sash. She rests against Becky who is gently brushing her hair.

BECKY

What would Miss Pinkerton say of us now? Two mothers-to-be in the midst of a war. Not quite what we studied in etiquette class.

AMELIA

Are you frightened? Of giving birth, I mean.

BECKY

You know me. I'm as tough as a nut. I'll probably have my baby after tea and dance at a ball the same evening.

AMELIA

I'm not frightened either. At least, not for myself. Just as long as George's child is well.

BECKY

You selfless little goose.

EXT. BALCONY. DAY.

The music of the pipes drifts down the street.

AMELIA

The bagpipes! But that means . . .

BECKY

Victory!

With a sob of relief, they embrace as, below, a column of Scottish soldiers marches into view—exhausted, wounded, proud, alive. Amelia's face is shining.

AMELIA

Thank you, Lord . . .

But as she looks up in thanks, ash from the burning town settles on her face, presaging death.

EXT. BATTLEFIELD. DAY

Here is the slaughter of Waterloo. Tree trunks blasted into stumps, the earth a clotted mass of flesh, mud and blood, and everywhere bodies and parts of bodies, human and equine, embedded in the slime. Death has rendered them, French and English, Belgium, Austrian, Prussian and Russian, young and not so young, identical. Children are scavenging for rings and buttons from the dead.

Behind a mound of earth, the camera comes to rest on a single figure, still in the dress uniform worn for a duchess's ball, one muddy arm flung out, eyes and mouth open and gaping in surprise at sudden death. It is, of course, our friend George Osborne.

CUT TO:

EXT. MILITARY CEMETERY OUTSIDE BRUSSELS. DAY.

Soldiers' bodies, a few in dress uniform like George's, are being wrapped in canvas and put into graves. At the far end of this military graveyard, the graves are already filled and marked by new wooden crosses. Old Mr Osborne walks down the grass aisle between them. He halts. A party has left one grave and is walking past him, Amelia and Becky in black, and Dobbin. Osborne turns away and then walks on towards the grave they were standing by.

DOBBIN

Mr Osborne! Mr Osborne!

Dobbin hurries towards him.

OSBORNE

Captain Dobbin or, I beg your pardon, Major Dobbin, since better men than you are dead and you step in their shoes.

DOBBIN

Better men *are* dead. I want to speak of one.

OSBORNE

Make it short, Sir.

DOBBIN

You are aware that his widow has been left a pauper?

OSBORNE

I do not know his widow. Nor wish to know her.

THE BATTLE OF WATERLOO: JUNE 18, 1815

In the novel *Vanity Fair,* one of the central characters, George Osborne, is killed during the battle of Waterloo. In reality, the battle was one of the central historical events of the nineteenth century as it effectively ended Napoleon's career and twenty-two years of European wars that had begun in 1793.

The Anglo-Dutch army was commanded by the Duke of Wellington, with the Prince of Orange nominally second-in-command. The core of their army was the British contingent. Wellington learned of Napoleon's invasion just before attending the Duchess of Richmond's ball in Brussels on June 15, but chose to continue the evening as normal, to prevent panic. The call to arms was sounded that night, and by the early hours of June 16, the entire army was on the march south from Brussels towards the French border. Wellington set his army in motion so quickly that some of the British officers had no time to change from their evening clothes.

The battle, fought twelve miles south of Brussels, continued throughout the day on June 18. Wellington was relying for final victory on the arrival of the Prussians, and late in the afternoon they appeared on the battlefield and entered the battle. From that moment the French forces started to collapse.

Casualties are estimated at 25,000 men killed and wounded, and 9,000 captured among the French forces.

DOBBIN
And what of his child? Will you not wish to know that?

This is a shock to the old man but he gathers his strength.

OSBORNE
It is just another consequence of George's disobedience and folly.

Dobbin understands that he will not make any headway. He takes an envelope out of his pocket.

DOBBIN
She would have me give you this.

OSBORNE
If it's a message from that woman, I do not want it.

DOBBIN
It is a message from your son, Sir. She has carried it for you from that day to this.

Osborne takes it, coldly, and Dobbin bows and goes. After a moment, Osborne opens the letter.

GEORGE (V.O.)
My dearest father, though we parted in anger, I want you to know that I will not disgrace you in the challenge that lies ahead—

Crumbling, Osborne covers his face with his hand and sobs.

OSBORNE
Oh, my boy . . . my darling boy . . .

INT. SEDLEY COTTAGE. FULHAM. AMELIA'S ROOM. DAY.
A healthy baby gurgles. Amelia leans over the cradle. She looks up. Dobbin is at the door. She smiles and whispers.

AMELIA
Shhh. Don't wake Georgy . . . Isn't he an angel?

DOBBIN
An angel.

AMELIA
When George died I wouldn't have believed there was room in my heart for anyone else. But see, he has absolute sovereignty.

Dobbin smiles sadly. These words bring him little hope.

AMELIA
We weren't expecting you today.

DOBBIN
I've come to tell you I have put in for a transfer. I embark next week for Bombay.

AMELIA
Bombay! Heavens. Why Bombay?

DOBBIN
Because it is as far away from here as I could manage.

At last he has her full attention.

AMELIA
I see.

DOBBIN
But before I leave I want to have one last try.

AMELIA
What sort of "try"?

He is impressive and dignified at this, his final, throw.

DOBBIN
I will resign my commission and I will stay in England. If you ask me to.

She is caught out by him.

AMELIA
If *I* ask you? But why should I—

DOBBIN
I will not go if you tell me not to.

His tone is so full of feeling, it is almost dangerous. For a moment they are silent.

AMELIA
You must see Jos when you get there.

She has given her answer. He nods. He has accepted it.

AMELIA
You'll let me write? To tell you how Georgy is doing? Dear William, you've been so good to him and me.

DOBBIN

The agents will forward any letters. Well, goodbye . . . We'll meet again one day.

AMELIA

Of course we will. Goodbye.

He turns at the door for one last look. As their eyes meet, they are both wondering whether she will regret her choice.

EXT. CURZON STREET HOUSE. DAY.
The landlord, Raggles, is with them, shaking Rawdon's hand.

RAGGLES

That's settled. You've made me a happy man. There's no tenant I'd rather have than a Crawley. Forty years I served your aunt and it still don't seem right to have a house without a Crawley in it.

RAWDON

It's been strange for me to have no Raggles about.

RAGGLES

You were always a wag, Colonel Rawdon, always Miss Crawley's favourite. Oh, I bricked those up against the window tax. Shall I have them opened for you?

But Rawdon wants no further outlay.

RAWDON

Window tax? I don't think so, thank you, Raggles. Sun isn't everything and Mrs Crawley looks very well by candlelight.

Raggles nods and goes. Rawdon stares at Crawley House.

RAWDON

Strange to be back in Curzon Street and not at Aunt Matilda's. Still . . . the house is a sound one and old Raggles is a good sort.

BECKY

He certainly is! We won't have to pay him a penny for months and think of the credit the address will give us!

There is something slightly troubling for Rawdon in this.

MONTAGE

Becky Sharp is coming to town. Rawdy makes his first appearance here with his nurse. Delivery carts arrive, upholsterers carrying in bolts of cloth, dealers bringing furniture and Becky is in the thick of it all. Her hair tied up and wearing an apron, she helps carry a rolled-up carpet and backing across the pavement, she falls on her bottom, shrieking with laughter. At just that moment, Lord Steyne rides by. The haughty nose tilts down. Their eyes meet and a faint smile twitches the corners of his mouth.

INT. CURZON STREET HOUSE. DRAWING ROOM. DAY.
Raggles is with them. Rawdon lies on a sofa in a half-furnished, half-decorated room. He is reading a letter. Becky has swatches of material which she is holding against the windows and furniture. Rawdon folds up the letter.

RAGGLES

I'm sorry to be the bearer of sad tidings, Colonel. You know how I esteemed your aunt. But there was no suffering. Mr Pitt and Lady Jane looked after her tenderly until the end.

BECKY

I'll bet they did.

RAGGLES

Right. Let me know if there's anything more I can do for you.

Raggles goes. Rawdon stands and walks to the window.

RAWDON

She's cut me out! I never thought she'd do it. And Pitt has swept the pool! Oh Becky, it's you and Rawdy I feel sorry for.

BECKY

Don't. Let it go.

RAWDON

And what now? When London has closed its doors on us?

BECKY

It'll come right. You'll see. We knew it wouldn't be easy. I'm a governess and you're a gambler. We were never going to shoot into Society. It'll take time.

RAWDON

What do we eat in the meanwhile?

BECKY

Oh my dear, let me manage that. We're Crawleys and Crawleys have credit. You'll be surprised to see how well we can live on practically nothing a year!

The door opens and the nursemaid appears with the baby.

NURSEMAID

Excuse me, Ma'am, but Master Rawdy has something to show you.

RAWDON

What is it, nurse?

For answer, she puts the boy down. He takes a few stumbling steps. At once Rawdon lies on the floor, arms outstretched.

RAWDON

Walking! And my word, if those aren't the stoutest steps I've ever seen a man take! You'll be marching to the colours in no time, my boy!

Rawdon watches his son walking. The image dissolves into . . .

EXT. HYDE PARK. DAY.

Rawdy, six years older, running towards a smart pony. His father catches him up and plants him in the saddle. Nearby another boy, Georgy, is with old Mr Sedley. He runs up.

GEORGY

Are you a soldier, Sir?

RAWDON

I am, my boy.

GEORGY

My Papa was a soldier, Sir. He fell at Waterloo.

RAWDON

I'm sorry to hear it. What was his name?

Sedley has drawn alongside. Now he speaks rather pompously.

SEDLEY

Captain George Osborne of the Ninth.

RAWDON

But I knew him well! I am Colonel Crawley and this is Rawdy. Tell me of George's wife, his dear, little wife. How is she?

SEDLEY

She is my daughter, Sir, and this my grandson, Georgy.

RAWDON

Then he shall have a ride.

He takes up the boy and seats him behind Rawdy.

SEDLEY

Look at them. You won't see a prettier pair, I think, this summer's day.

They fall into step together as a landau passes. With a start, the passenger catches sight of Sedley and the boys. It is Maria Osborne. The dialogue continues as voice-over.

SEDLEY (V.O.)

Take my card, Sir. Perhaps we might do some business. I have a few interests of my own . . .

RAWDON (V.O.)

Indeed? Well, when I am next looking to invest some capital, I see I must consult you.

SEDLEY (V.O.)

You could do worse, Sir . . .

EXT. CURZON STREET HOUSE. DAY.

A dour looking man waits on the step.

INT. CURZON STREET HOUSE. DRAWING ROOM. DAY.

Becky and Rawdon are eating at a small table in the window near a pretty, lady's desk. The food is clearly not good.

RAWDON

Dash it, Becky. Is this really the best we can manage?

BECKY

There's my desk and here's the key. If you can find a spare penny piece in it, I take my hat off to you. Unless you mean for once to make a contribution?

RAWDON

Don't be hard on me, old girl. I've had a bad run. Things'll get better . . . . Ugh. You'd think the whole animal was made of scrag end.

BECKY

If only the butcher didn't want to be paid. How can he be so selfish?

She catches Rawdon's eye, laughing, defusing his guilt. A footman comes in. His manner is insolent, even frightening.

FOOTMAN

That Mr Moss is here. I've brought him up.

RAWDON

Then take him down again, damn you. Until we've finished eating.

But an equally threatening Moss is already in the room.

MOSS

Needs must, Colonel. And I hope you've got good news for me.

BECKY

I'm sorry, Mr Moss, but we're not magicians. We can't give you money if we haven't got it.

MOSS

Why not? You can spend it when you haven't got it.

BECKY

You're wasted as a bailiff. You should write for the stage.

MOSS

And you should go on it for you're a good enough actress.

RAWDON

That's enough! We cannot pay you and there it is. Now get out!

MOSS

All right, I'll go but I'll be back. And when I am, you'd best have something for me.

INT. SIR PITT'S BEDROOM - NIGHT

Horrocks is preparing some tincture in this dank and chaotic room. There is a sound from the pile of blankets on a vast and dilapidated four poster. Horrocks takes up his candle and carries the full glass over.

HORROCKS

Here is your medicine, Sir Pitt.

But the old man waves the glass away.

SIR PITT

Take it away. There's no medicine to cure what ails me. I'm dying, Horrocks. This is the end.

HORROCKS

Come, Sir Pitt—

SIR PITT

It's the end, I tell you.

HORROCKS

Shall I fetch Mr Pitt? Or the doctor?

SIR PITT

Or the lawyer? That's the question, Horrocks. Pitt's had Tilly's money. Shall he have mine, too? Or should it go to Rawdon? And to foxy little Becky?

HORROCKS

I can fetch the lawyer if you want me to, sir.

Sir Pitt thinks for a moment, then shakes his head.

SIR PITT

Nay. Let Pitt have it all. He's a pompous beggar but he'll keep the old place together when Rawdon would throw it to the dogs. Give Rawdon my love but let Pitt keep the money.

And the old man sinks back onto his pillow exhausted.

INT. DRAWING ROOM. QUEEN'S CRAWLEY. DAY.
Pitt, busy with his pamphlets, is with Jane and her mother.

LADY SOUTHDOWN

Ask them here? Then I must leave at once! Have the goodness to order the horses!

JANE

Mama, we cannot know that what is said of her is just or even true. And now Sir Pitt is dead, they must come for his funeral, surely.

LADY SOUTHDOWN

But . . . not both of them!

PITT

That marriage, Madam, gave me my aunt's fortune. Should I cry out against it now?

LADY SOUTHDOWN

Well, I never thought to be turned from my own daughter's door!

She sweeps out. Pitt calls after her.

PITT

Don't forget your medicine chest!

Jane looks to Pitt but he shakes his head.

PITT

She won't go. She has spent last year's dividends. I cannot see her in a hotel in Bournemouth.

EXT. QUEEN'S CRAWLEY. DRAWING ROOM. DAY.

The company, all in mourning, are going into luncheon. Including Lady Southdown. Becky is with the girls.

BECKY

And your piano practice? I hope you have not been neglecting it.

ROSE

No, Miss Shar— Mrs Crawley.

BECKY

I'm glad to hear it. You must play for me.

She passes on through the door.

JANE

See? No airs. No bid to bury her governess past. You cannot dislike her for that, surely.

LADY SOUTHDOWN

No. I agree. Not for that.

INT. QUEEN'S CRAWLEY. GREAT HALL. EVE.

They're near the end of lunch. The two boys are with them.

LADY SOUTHDOWN

Mrs Crawley, when you told Miss Crawley your mother was a Montmorency—

BECKY

I never said that. I talked once of the Montmorencys but that's all. She must have misunderstood me. My mother sang opera.

LADY SOUTHDOWN

I see . . .

Becky has made even Lady Southdown feel guilty.

PITT

What shall we do after dinner?

BECKY

Well, we are in mourning . . .

PITT

You are right to query me but I do not think my father's death should banish *all* social converse.

Becky is scoring huge points all round.

BECKY

Then what I should like best would be to play something with our little boys.

This is aimed straight at Jane's heart. It hits the target.

JANE

Little Pitt has not been well.

BECKY

Many children are peaky at that age. Rawdy was the same and yet look at him now!

This is news to both Rawdon and Rawdy.

LADY SOUTHDOWN

I gave little Pitt some tonic before dinner.

JANE

I wonder if you do not give him too much tonic sometimes, Mama.

BECKY

I remember how your medicines helped poor Miss Crawley.

This second mention send a *frisson* through the room.

PITT

We are family and so I may speak out. I hope that Aunt Matilda's final disposition has not . . .

He tails off rather lamely. Becky speaks.

BECKY

Miss Crawley gave me the best husband in the world. How could I be angry with her? I'm glad her fortune will restore the glory of this place and this family of which I'm proud to be a member.

An approving silence greets this. Then:

PITT

It is we Crawleys, Madam, who are the gainers by your marriage.

This earns a dazzling smile around the table.

EXT. INDIAN VERANDAH. NIGHT.

Dobbin sits at a desk in the lamp light with the sounds of India all around him. He is writing a letter.

DOBBIN (V.O.)

How are you, my dear Amelia, and how is all your little family?

He puts down his pen and strolls along the verandah. A family scene is enacted before him as a young father helps his wife rearrange her slipping veil. She smiles her thanks and takes their young son's hand in hers . . . Dobbin returns to his desk.

DOBBIN (V.O.)

If you did but know how brightly your image burns for me, how I dream of you and Georgy hand in hand. Every detail of your daily life is precious to me as I sit and write beneath the Indian sun.

EXT. QUEEN'S CRAWLEY. POND. DAY.

Rawdy is riding a pony. His sickly cousin watching with Jane and Rawdon. Something is troubling the child.

LITTLE PITT

Mama, where has Grandpapa gone?

JANE

He is in Heaven, darling.

Rawdon clears his throat either in hope or disbelief.

LITTLE PITT

Will I ever see him again?

JANE

One day. One day we will all see him again.

LITTLE PITT

Will it be soon, Mama?

Jane cannot answer this but Rawdy has trotted over.

RAWDY

Would you like a ride? I will hold you quite safe.

LITTLE PITT

May I, Mama?

JANE

Of course, my darling.

As the two ride round, Jane watches her sad little boy and her eyes fill with tears. Rawdon looks at her with pity.

RAWDON

No one warns you how much you're going to love them, do they, Ma'am?

Jane is too moved to speak, but she takes his arm. She and Rawdon have each found their ally. Nearby, Becky is witness to this perfect family scene in which she plays no part.

INT. DINING ROOM. OSBORNE HOUSE. DAY.

Osborne is dining alone with his daughter in this tomb-like chamber. They eat in silence as the footmen tiptoe about.

OSBORNE

What is the matter with you?

MARIA

Nothing, Father.

But she fumbles her spoon and drops it on the plate.

OSBORNE

For Heaven's sake! Out with it!

Mr. Osborne is a blinkered man who's put all his money and his time and energy into making money. He has no sympathy for anyone who is poor. He is a selfish, sometimes unpleasant man, but he loves his son desperately—it's the only light in his life. His story springs from that central relationship. Mira wanted to bring out the vulnerability of his character—his sentimentalism as well as his obstinate strength which was more obvious. —Jim Broadbent

MARIA

It is only that I was driving in the park the other day and . . .

OSBORNE

And?

Partly through terror of him, she starts to cry.

MARIA

Oh Father! I've seen little George! He was with Mr Sedley and I knew him at once. He's as beautiful as an angel and . . . so like him!

She weeps but he does not reprimand her. Instead he lifts his soup spoon but his hand is shaking. The loud clock ticks.

EXT. SEDLEY COTTAGE. FULHAM. NIGHT.

A beggar child runs out of the way of a great carriage that looms out of the mist and clatters to a halt. The horses stamp and snort their ghostly breath. A man approaches the door. We see his back as he raises his hand.

INT. SEDLEY COTTAGE. FULHAM. NIGHT.
Amelia is sewing a child's shirt. There is a knock.

MRS SEDLEY

Whoever can that be?

EXT. SEDLEY COTTAGE. FULHAM. NIGHT.

Amelia opens the door and starts. It is Mr Osborne.

OSBORNE

This is really your home then?

AMELIA

It is.

OSBORNE

How is such a thing possible?

AMELIA

What do you want with me, Sir?

OSBORNE

I have a proposal to put to you.

EXT/INT. COACH. DAY.

The Crawleys wave them away from Queen's Crawley.

145

RAWDY
I like Aunt Jane. Don't you Papa?

RAWDON
I do. Pitt's lucky there. She's kind and good.

BECKY
I could be good on five thousand a year.

RAWDON
Do you not care for her, then?

BECKY
What does that matter? Don't you see what this means? We are back in the family! The first barrier is gone. At long last we have begun!

Hugging herself with dreams of the future, she leans back.

EXT. SEDLEY COTTAGE. FULHAM. DAY.
Mrs Sedley is seated on an old chair. Amelia is pulling up vegetables. Georgy looks at his mother working.

GEORGY
Why do you do that, Mama? It is so degrading.

AMELIA
I do it so we may eat. Hunger is degrading, too.

He starts to kick a turnip that has rolled to his feet.

AMELIA
That is our food, Georgy. It is not your toy.

GEORGY
I hate our food! And I have no toys! None that I want anyway!

He storms off into the house.

"I have seen George! He is as beautiful as an angel—and so like him!" The old man opposite her did not say a word, but flushed up and began to tremble in every limb.

—William Makepeace Thackeray, *Vanity Fair*, 1847

MRS SEDLEY
How can you be so cruel?

This is an astonishing charge.

AMELIA
Cruel?

MRS SEDLEY
When he might have had the finest education money can buy? When he could have been as rich as a lord? And his own mother steals his future because she wants to tuck him up in bed!

AMELIA
Mama, "a mother's love is more than any Mayfair palace." Do you not remember what Major Dobbin wrote?

MRS SEDLEY
Pray don't let's talk of Major Dobbin.

AMELIA
Why ever not?

MRS SEDLEY
What is the point now he's engaged?

AMELIA
What?

Mrs Sedley is enjoying her daughter's shock.

MRS SEDLEY
Did you not read Joseph's letter? *The Major is engaged to a Miss Glorvina O'Dowd.*

Amelia is too surprised to speak.

MRS SEDLEY
Well, what did you expect? Sending him off to Timbuktu? The man who might have given us all a decent life. That's a daughter's love, I suppose!

AMELIA
Mama, I don't see why I should sacrifice myself for your comfort when your son—

MRS SEDLEY
Just because Joseph forgets his duty is no reason for you to!

AMELIA
But how could I betray George when —

MRS SEDLEY
Pshaw! George! What idiocy is this? That in his blessed memory your parents must starve and you make your own child a beggar!

This time even Amelia cannot defend her choices.

INT. SEDLEY COTTAGE. AMELIA'S BEDROOM. NIGHT.
Georgy is in his little bed. Amelia's school trunk, old and battered now, is neatly packed. The "A.S." has been crossed out and replaced with "G.O." George's remaining things are stacked near, ready for departure. Amelia reads from a Bible.

AMELIA
. . .and Naomi said unto Ruth, Go, return to your father's house. The Lord deal kindly with you as ye have dealt with me—

GEORGY
There'll be much more room there for all my things. Won't there?

AMELIA
Much . . .

GEORGY
And can I get a proper pencil-case?

AMELIA
I'm sure.

GEORGY
Oh well then.

He lies back content as his mother continues.

AMELIA
Then Ruth said Entreat me not to leave thee or not to follow after thee. For whither thou goest, I will go, thy people shall be my people and thy God my God—

A sudden, marvellous thought occurs to the boy.

GEORGY
Will I have a pony, Mama?

Amelia nods, controlling her tears as she resumes the tale.

EXT. CURZON STREET. DAY.
Moss and his henchmen are putting articles from the house into a cart under the gaze of servants and neighbours.

MOSS
Careful of that table. That's valuable, that is.

There is a cry. Becky is running down the street.

BECKY
What do you think you're doing?

MOSS
Told you I'd be back, lady . . . Better wrap that looking glass—

BECKY
How dare you!

She seizes hold of the little desk where we know she kept her money. The man and Moss pull the other end.

MOSS
Let go, lady, or I'll call the constable!

BECKY
You can call the King for all I care! You're not having that!

The two teams grunt and strain against each other as a silver topped cane slams down onto the surface of the desk.

STEYNE (V.O.)
I wonder if I might be of help.

Mira is one of the few directors I've ever worked with who tells the extras what's actually happening on set. She realizes that there's not a corner of the frame that's not important, that as a spectator your eye is going to wander and that all details contribute to the whole. Not only is she technically competent but in terms of little minor details and the tiny moments where drama is created, she's hyper aware of these—a look, a pause, a quickening of rhythm, an overlap. I would say that Mira Nair, in terms of directing actors, is one of the best. —Gabriel Byrne

Moss looks up to find the source of the voice. At the sight of Steyne, he lets the little desk clatter to the pavement.

INT. CURZON STREET HOUSE. DRAWING ROOM. DAY.

Moss counts the last of the notes and pockets them.

MOSS

Pleasure doing business.

BECKY

Just go.

He does. Becky is left alone with the Marquess of Steyne who leans calmly against the chimneypiece.

STEYNE

We meet at last.

BECKY

I know you, Lord Steyne, though you do not know me. You will have forgotten but you were kind to my father once. Many years ago.

STEYNE

Indeed. You intrigue me. I am seldom praised for being kind.

Looking into his cold, grey eyes, it is easy to believe.

STEYNE

What was his name?

BECKY

Francis Sharp. He was a painter and you bought his work when no one else would. It kept us afloat for a time.

STEYNE

You are Francis Sharp's daughter! But I have several of his works. He'd a great talent for painting as I recall and none at all for life.

BECKY

I'm attempting to redress that balance. It is my challenge.

STEYNE

I have watched you in the lists and I wish you luck for it will not be easy. Of course it's the women who keep the doors of Society closed. They do not like outsiders to discover there is nothing behind them.

He watches her for a moment. Then he makes up his mind.

STEYNE

Should you like to come to Gaunt House?

BECKY

Very much, my lord.

STEYNE

You will be bored there. My wife is as gay as Lady Macbeth and my daughters-in-law as cheerful as Goneril and Regan. They will bully you and snub you and patronise you. But it's what you want, I suppose.

BECKY

It is.

He takes out another note and hands it to her.

STEYNE

You had better take this. You don't want him back tomorrow.

She looks at it and raises her eyebrows then, without a word, she goes to the desk which is back in its place. She unlocks it, puts in the note and locks it again.

INT. CURZON ST. HOUSE. BEDROOM. DAY.

BECKY

Lace me up.

RAWDON

You're playing with fire, Becky.

BECKY

Dearest, be reasonable. Now that society is smiling upon us at last.

RAWDON

You can pander all you like to the Great and Good, but I know them all—we're not their type and never will be.

BECKY

Of course we are! You've the best blood in England in your veins if you'd only use it! You know Lord Steyne is planning a dinner next week with the Minister of War, and promises to talk of nothing but you. The cards are in your hand, darling. Must I show you how to play them?

RAWDON

So now you're to instruct me in games of chance?

BECKY

I just want you to think on the winnings.

RAWDON

I know what we have to win, I'm just afraid of what we might lose. You're taking favours from a tiger, Becky

BECKY

I'm not afraid.

RAWDON

I don't doubt it. Keep your eyes open.

INT. GAUNT HOUSE. BREAKFAST ROOM. DAY.

In this cold, splendid, marble room three ladies are at breakfast. Steyne is with them.

STEYNE

Must I repeat myself? You will write a card to Colonel and Mrs Crawley.

LADY STEYNE

But Blanche writes them . . .

LADY GAUNT

Not this time, I don't.

STEYNE

Lady Steyne, I cannot believe I am compelled to issue a request three times.

There is a silence. At last, Lady Steyne, nods.

LADY STEYNE

I will write it.

LADY GAUNT

Then I will not be present. I will go home.

STEYNE

Good. Stay there. Let me be free your damned tragedy airs. Who are you to give orders? You're here to have children and you're barren! My son is sick of you! There's no one in the family who doesn't wish you dead!

The ferocity of the attack is shocking. His voice softens.

STEYNE

Besides, what is the matter with Mrs Crawley? She's not very well born, it's true, but she's no worse than Fanny's illustrious ancestor, the first de la Jones.

LADY GEORGE

The money I brought into this family, Sir—

STEYNE

Purchased my second son as a husband when all the world knows he is *mad!* Enough! This is my house! If I invite the trash from every prison and brothel in London, you will receive them and make them welcome.

He goes, leaving three battered women in their gilded cage.

INT. CURZON STREET HOUSE. DRAWING ROOM. DAY.

A hand places a written card with the Steyne crest in the looking glass.

INT. CURZON STREET HOUSE. DRAWING ROOM. DAY.
Rawdon is playing with his son, tossing him in the air.

RAWDON

That's a fine boy!

He throws him up again but this time the child hits his head on the ceiling. He is opening his mouth to cry.

RAWDON

For God's sake, Rawdy, don't wake Mama!

The child hesitates, watching his father plead.

RAWDON

She's sleeping, resting for a dinner tonight . . . Please!

The urgency convinces the boy. Rawdon hugs him.

RAWDON

Jove, but you're a plucky chap!

It is however clear that now Rawdon is frightened of Becky.

INT. GAUNT HOUSE. DINING ROOM. NIGHT.

About twenty guests have finished dinner. They are leaving the room as Lord Steyne approaches Becky.

STEYNE

Now comes the test. We men go to the smoking room while you must join the ladies. Good luck.

Becky Sharp is a singer. This is her gift....and her passport to the higher realms of London society. We began with this premise for the music in the movie. Before production began, Mira approached me with two poems by Thackeray's contemporaries: Lord Byron's "She Walks in Beauty" and Tennyson's "The Crimson Petal." Mira and I had collaborated before, albeit in the different cultural worlds of *Kama Sutra* and *Monsoon Wedding*. Mira's sensitivity to music and her exquisite taste in vocals and lyrics had been hallmarks of our previous work together, and so I was thrilled to have the task of setting these poems to music that would sum up the power and transcendent quality of Becky's gift of song. A gift which Becky has no hesitation to sell, or use in any way to move herself forward. The selling out of what is irreplaceably valuable is one of the themes of the film, and one therefore imbedded in the music itself. And songs map out Becky's journey: from the innocent beginning of Byron's girlish song (sung by Norwegian-born Sissel) over the head credit sequence, to the final scene, when Becky arrives, in triumphal Indian procession (to the song of Shankar, Elsan and Loy), an Indianized pop song based on the orchestral theme of the film. Thackeray, who was born in Imperial India, was steeped in the idea of the relationship between Empire and colonies, and so en route we feature Assalaam Alaikum by Egyptian artist Hakim, as well as other threads of South Asian and Far Eastern sounds that were (and are) woven into the fabric of the Empire. The adventure of recording a modern day feature film score meant that we worked in hotel rooms and studios in three different continents (at least) and recording with a south Indian percussionist, an early music singer from Virginia, a harpsichordist from Glasgow, and the Philharmonia Orchestra of London, among others. —Mychael Danna, Composer

NOW SLEEPS THE CRIMSON PETAL
Alfred Lord Tennyson

Now sleeps the crimson petal, now the white;
Nor waves the cypress in the palace walk;
Nor winks the gold fin in the porphyry font:
The firefly wakens: waken thou with me.

Now droops the milkwhite peacock like a ghost,
And like a ghost she glimmers on to me.

Now lies the Earth all Danae to the stars,
And all thy heart lies open unto me.

Now slides the silent meteor on, and leaves
A shining furrow, as thy thoughts in me.

Now folds the lily all her sweetness up,
And slips into the bosom of the lake:
So fold thyself, my dearest, thou, and slip
Into my bosom and be lost in me.

Despite herself, Becky looks apprehensively at the door through which the women are walking.

> STEYNE
> Remember. You have no friends beyond that door.

INT. GAUNT HOUSE. DRAWING ROOM. NIGHT.
Becky is clearly having a tough time. The women are mostly gathered at a table, looking at drawings. Becky joins them.

> BECKY
> Lady Bareacres, what did you make of the new *Figaro?* I thought it—

Lady Bareacres smiles coolly and moves away.

> *BECKY*
> *Are you interested in drawings, Lady Gaunt, because I—*

> *LADY GAUNT*
> *Not very.*

She too drifts off. Becky is alone at the table. She covers her discomfort by studying some sketches. The women gather at the chimneypiece. Becky follows but before she gets there, the women have gone again. This time to pretend to admire a painting on the far side. Lady Steyne has been watching.

LADY STEYNE

I hear that you sing and play very beautifully, Mrs Crawley. I wish you would be kind enough to play for me.

Lady Gaunt hisses under her breath.

LADY GAUNT

What are you doing?

LADY STEYNE

I've seen enough cruelty in this house not to want to inflict it.

Becky sits down and starts to play, falteringly at first but with gathering confidence. Her voice is amazing and gradually the other women take Lady Steyne's lead until at last Lady Gaunt stands alone. The doors open and the men join the ladies. Steyne approaches the piano.

STEYNE

You have survived, then?

BECKY

Only because your wife threw me a rope.

Steyne looks about and finds his wife. He bows courteously and smiles. Becky's playing ends. After a moment of silence, Lady Steyne starts to applaud. The others follow.

STEYNE

It is enough. You are through the door.

INT/EXT. MONTAGE.

Smartly dressed men arrive at the Curzon Street door, held open by a liveried footman. As the camera drifts over to the windows, Becky is revealed singing at the piano, watched by Steyne. During this we become aware of Wenham, Steyne's familiar. Society has come to Becky's house, forcing its way up and down the cramped stairs, laughing to find each other there. A hypnotist tries to put a guest into a trance amid shrieks of merriment. Becky's entertaining is up to the minute! Meanwhile, the looking glass, starting with one or two dreary cards jammed into its

frame, is gradually filled until, by the end, the mantleshelf is bulging. Meanwhile, Rawdon hovers, drinking too much, gambling too much, lost. Rawdy watches through the open door as his mother sings. Steyne looks up, sees him and walks over to shut the door. A footman looks sympathetically at the boy.

RAWDY

I wish she'd sing for me.

EXT. HYDE PARK. DAY.

Becky is bowling along Rotten Row in Steyne's carriage.

STEYNE

That boy of yours, when does he go away to school?

BECKY

When he's older, I suppose.

STEYNE

No, no. He must learn to stand on his own two feet at once. Miss that lesson in childhood and you'll miss it all your life.

BECKY

I'm not sure Rawdon could spare him yet—

STEYNE

I will arrange it. No need to thank me.

He gazes at the passing carriages.

STEYNE

Perhaps then we could see a little more of each other.

She laughs trying to make a joke of it. He does not smile.

BECKY

Aren't you forgetting my husband?

STEYNE

I never forget anything, Mrs Crawley. Least of all an unpaid debt.

This does not have a calming effect.

EXT. CURZON STREET HOUSE. DAY.

Rawdy joins his parents where a coach is waiting.

RAWDY

Must I go? Must I really?

RAWDON

But Rawdy, it's for your own sake . . . You know what they say—there's no better start in life than a sound education.

BECKY

And you'll have such fun with the other boys.

RAWDY

Can't I stay if I promise to be good?

The thought that the boy thinks he is being punished nearly kills Rawdon who crouches before him. Rawdy looks into his father's eyes. There are tears there. Rawdon struggles on.

RAWDON

It won't be for long, old chap.

RAWDY

Yes, it will.

EXT. OSBORNE HOUSE. DAY.

It is cold and windy. Amelia sits huddled in a shawl watching the front of the splendid Osborne house when Georgy emerges with his grandfather. They start towards the carriage.

GEORGY

Mother?

He runs across, followed more slowly by Osborne.

GEORGY

Mother, what are you doing here? I was coming to see you on Saturday.

AMELIA

I had some business nearby and . . .

GEORGY

It's a grand house, isn't it?

AMELIA

Yes . . . I knew it well once.

She cannot speak for fear of weeping. The old man arrives, glowering. She is quick to explain her presence.

AMELIA

I made Georgy some shirts. I was going to leave them for him.

She opens a brown paper package with the shirts inside.

GEORGY

Oh, mother! I couldn't wear your funny old shirts now!

AMELIA

No . . . I suppose not.

OSBORNE

Do some good. Give them to a beggar. Good day to you, Madam.

He goes, beckoning to the haughty little boy.

GEORGY

You are silly, Mama.

AMELIA

Yes. Silly old Mama.

She wraps up her offering as she watches them walk away.

EXT. LONDON STREET. DAY.

Amelia, in misery, walks blindly along. She crosses the street and has to jump back from a coach as it whirls past. She has not seen it holds the wretched Rawdy.

INT. OFFICERS' EXERCISE ROOM. INDIA. DAY.

Dobbin is waiting, dressed for wrestling. A servant enters.

SERVANT

A letter for you, Major.

Dobbin thanks him and takes it. At once he knows and relishes the writing. Looking about, he finds a paper knife on a writing table and opens it.

AMELIA (V.O.)

Dear William, thank you for your letter which took three months to reach me but was very welcome when it did. Georgy is in good health but living with his grandfather—

This jolts him.

DOBBIN

What!

OFFICER (V.O.)

Dobbin? Are you ready?

His wrestling partner has arrived, similarly dressed.

DOBBIN

Ready.

But he cannot resist a further glance at the letter.

AMELIA (V.O.)

I am persuaded it is better so—for his sake—and I must submit.

DOBBIN

Nonsense!

OFFICER

Dobs, if you'd rather leave it for some other time, I can easily find—

DOBBIN

No, no. I'm coming.

But again he looks down.

AMELIA (V.O.)

I confess it was with quite a pang that I read Joseph's news of your engagement but I want to add my—

DOBBIN

What!!!

Putting the letter down, he turns to his opponent and in one movement flings him to the ground, throwing himself on top of him and holding him in a stranglehold. The man gasps for air.

OFFICER

Dobs! Dobs! I can't breathe!

Looking down, Dobbin is surprised to find an apparently dying man beneath his arm. He releases his victim to rub his neck.

OFFICER

Good Lord, Dobs! What in Heaven's name's got into you?

When Dobbin speaks, it is with absolute decision.

DOBBIN

It's time I returned to England.

EXT. GAUNT HOUSE. NIGHT.

Flares burn either side of the entrance. Carriages arrive.

INT. GAUNT HOUSE. DRAWING ROOM. NIGHT.

The room has been converted into an eastern tent. The King is there with Pitt and Jane, the Bareacres, the Darlingtons and other familiar faces. Steyne nods across at his right man, Mr Wenham, who signals for a gong and addresses the company.

WENHAM

Your Majesty, my lords, ladies and gentlemen, will you take your seats? The entertainment is about to begin.

The company start to stroll towards the gilded chairs.

BAREACRES

What has Steyne got planned, Lady Steyne?

LADY STEYNE

I wish I knew.

With a clash of cymbals, Lord Steyne appears on the stage.

KING

Come along, Lord Steyne. You have kept your secret long enough. What have you got for us?

STEYNE

Never fear, Sir. All will be revealed.

He claps his hands. A huge pair of curtains pull back and music strikes up. A group of dancers come on in eastern costumes, among them Lady Gaunt and Lady George. They are not enjoying themselves. Steyne whispers as they pass.

STEYNE

Come, my dears, smile. For I should hate to be angry with you.

Mechanically, they pull the corners of their mouths up. He remains on the edge of the stage, enjoying his creation.

BAREACRES

Just look! Steyne the Pasha with his nautch girls!

The chorus is in place. A new, veiled dancer comes spinning down the line. Her costume is more revealing and her dancing more fascinating than the others. There is a gasp.

BAREACRES

Good God! It's Mrs Crawley!

DARLINGTON

Then Steyne wasn't lying. All is revealed.

They laugh and then notice that Rawdon is just behind them. He moves away in a silent fury to join Pitt and Jane.

DARLINGTON

Poor old Crawley. What a duffer she's made of him.

The dance continues to a wild, dazzling conclusion. The dancers move forward to receive their applause and then step down from the dais to join the company.

KING

Well done, Lady Gaunt. I had not seen you as an Eastern exotic.

LADY GAUNT

Nor I, Sir . . . If you will forgive me, I must change before dinner.

At a nod from Steyne, Wenham has brought Becky into the King's orbit. The King catches sight of her.

KING

Ah, Mrs Crawley. Lady Gaunt, will you make the presentation?

LADY GAUNT

But I must go upstairs and change—

KING

At once, Lady Gaunt.

LADY GAUNT

Of course, Your Majesty. May I present Mrs Rawdon Crawley.

The words are ashes in her mouth. Becky sinks into a fluid court curtsey to be raised from it by the King's own hand.

KING

Well, Mrs Crawley. To the victor the spoils. You have carried off our hearts in triumph.

BECKY

If that is so, then Your Majesty may rest easy that your heart will be well looked after.

He throws back his head and laughs.

KING

That's a relief for it has been bruised in its time. You must tell me at dinner how you mean to treat it. You will sit next to me.

LADY GAUNT

The precedence would make that a little difficult, Sir.

KING

I am the King, Lady Gaunt. I confer precedence.

He turns away leaving the watching Steyne to enjoy the squashing of his reviled and humiliated daughter-in-law.

EXT. GAUNT HOUSE. BALCONY. NIGHT.

Becky, dressed normally and wonderfully again, is on the balcony with Steyne. The garden below twinkles with light.

STEYNE

Well, are you happy? I said I would make you Queen of the Night and I have.

She looks out over the great city.

BECKY

I am certainly grateful, my lord.

STEYNE

But not happy? Ah . . . well, which of us is happy? Which of us has his desire or, having it, is satisfied?

BECKY

Not you? You take pleasures in your pictures, surely.

STEYNE

Yes. *They shelter me.* I can hide behind them.

BECKY

You, my lord, hide from what?

STEYNE

From the truth known to every shepherd and footman: that the only thing of value is to love and be loved. I hide from it because I did not think that I would ever find it, but now . . . .

He takes Becky's face in his hands.

STEYNE

I do believe I have.

BECKY

You jest with me, my Lord. I make a poor companion with the splendors that surround you.

STEYNE

How foolish I must appear if you think the gilded geejaws of my love have satisfied me. The chief advantage of being born into Society is that one learns early what a tawdry puppet play it is.

As he speaks, they move into the drawing room. She stops. The picture of her mother, *Virtue Betrayed*, is before her. She stares at it and he stares at her. She strokes the painted surface, sensing the trap closing around her.

STEYNE

Do you remember the child who set a high price on it before she could bear to see it go?

BECKY

Not high enough.

STEYNE

The trouble is, Mrs Crawley, you have taken the goods. It is too late to query the price.

As he moves towards her, she sees again the picture. The horror of the painting's heroine at her predicament seems to chime with what it is witnessing now. Becky closes her eyes to shut out the image.

Through the open door, Rawdon watches his wife with Steyne. With a muttered oath, he storms away down the stairs.

INT. GAUNT HOUSE. HALL.

At the foot of the stair, Rawdon runs into Mr Wenham.

WENHAM

Going, Crawley? I'll walk with you.

EXT. CURZON STREET. NIGHT.

They stroll away from Gaunt House. Suddenly, Moss steps out of the shadows with his usual thugs in attendance.

MOSS

Good evening, Colonel.

Rawdon turns to run but Wenham blocks his path.

MOSS

It's only a small thing, Colonel. One hundred and sixty five pounds at the suit of a Mr Nathan.

RAWDON

Lend me a hundred, Wenham, for God's sake. I've got seventy at home.

WENHAM

I've not ten pounds in the world, my dear fellow, but don't worry. You'll look after him, won't you, Moss?

MOSS

How can you ask, Mr Wenham? I run the most comfortable debtor's prison in London. Ask anyone.

WENHAM

There you are, Crawley. He can't say fairer than that. G'night.

He turns towards Gaunt House as Rawdon is led to a cab.

INT. MOSS'S PRIVATE PRISON. NIGHT.

Rawdon sits, disconsolate and alone, in a dingy room, dirty and threadbare. The door opens and Moss looks in.

MOSS

Sure I can't get you anything, Colonel?

RAWDON

My wife will be here any moment.

MOSS

If you say so, Sir. Ring the bell when you want something. It's your old bed and it's well aired.

RAWDON

You did deliver my letter?

MOSS

Put it into her hand, Sir. Is there no one else I might call on?

RAWDON

My brother, I suppose. But I hardly like to trouble him when I know Becky will be here before too long.

MOSS

Even so, sir.

Rawdon goes to write another note. He stops.

RAWDON

It must be taking her some time to raise the money.

MOSS

That's what it must be, Sir.

INT. CURZON STREET HOUSE. DRAWING ROOM. NIGHT.

Becky holds Rawdon's letter. Steyne is with her.

BECKY

Poor Rawdon . . .

STEYNE

Colonel Crawley will be well enough. One night won't kill him. Heaven knows he's on familiar territory. Shall we go up?

He is growing impatient but how Becky doesn't want to!

INT. MOSS'S PRIVATE PRISON. NIGHT.

A hooded figure is walking through the dank corridor with Moss. The single lamp throws grotesque shadows. A door is unlocked. Rawdon lies on the bed. He springs up.

RAWDON

Becky! Thank God!

But it is not Becky.

JANE

It is I, Rawdon. It is Jane. Pitt is away so when your note came I read it. I have paid Mr Moss.

Rawdon takes her hand, meaning to thank her, but instead he starts to cry. After a while he recovers, shaking his head.

RAWDON

This is no place for a woman like you. You should not have come here. I am not worth it.

JANE

Yes, you are. You are my brother now and I know you are a brother I can be proud of.

Her genuine goodness has overpowered him.

RAWDON

I want to change, Jane. I mean to make a different life. For me and Rawdy. At least I mean to try.

JANE

Then, you will succeed. Now, get your things and I'll take you home.

INT. CURZON STREET HOUSE. BECKY'S BEDROOM. NIGHT.

Steyne is in his shirtsleeves. Becky is at the door.

STEYNE

I am sorry, my dear. You must forgive my excess of zeal.

BECKY

You need no forgiveness from me.

STEYNE

But I do. I need your forgiveness and your love.

He is close to her, stroking her face.

His tender tone is hardening into something frightening.

BECKY

Suppose my wish is to finish now? If I ask no other favour?

Steyne looks at her with his cold, terrifying eyes.

STEYNE

You've had your wishes, Mrs Crawley.

He has indeed waited long enough and savagely he pulls her down clamping his mouth to hers. He thrusts his hand into her bosom, tearing the material as he does so. She fights back but she is no match for his strength. He is on her. He pushes his hand roughly beneath her skirts . . . .

Rawdon is like a bright diamond at the beginning of the film but as the story unfolds he loses his sheen. He loves life and has a tremendous joie de vivre but during the course of the film he sags, deflates, and loses his shine, taking to drinking and gambling. He becomes a little lost because he is married to a woman with a rapacious ambition for social climbing. He didn't realize how addicted to that mode of living she was. When he finally discovers that she's betrayed him by not paying the debt to get him out of prison he is really broken by it. It's a sad idea that this man who really felt that he had found his soul mate discovers that she has betrayed him, and that breaks his heart. The love he has for his little boy Rawdy is what finally keeps him human.

—James Purefoy

There is a sound on the landing. They barely have time to spring apart when the door opens and Rawdon enters. Steyne at once seizes his coat and starts to put it on.

STEYNE

Crawley! What kept you?

He starts to wipe imaginary sweat from his brow. Rawdon is stock still with fury. Becky now runs to him.

BECKY

Nothing happened! Rawdon, I beg you to believe me! I am innocent!

Still Rawdon is immobile. Suddenly, Steyne suspects a trap. He looks about him.

STEYNE

What is this? What scheming are you both up to?

Becky is not listening. She turns to Steyne.

BECKY

Tell him I am innocent!

This is too much.

STEYNE

You! Innocent! When I bought every trinket on your body! Let me pass, Sir!

With something like a roar, Rawdon seizes him.

RAWDON

You cowardly, villainous *liar!*

But Steyne is not a weakling and he fights back, pushing Rawdon out through the door towards the stairs.

INT. CURZON STREET HOUSE. STAIRCASE. NIGHT.
Becky, terrified and awestruck, follows as they fight.

BECKY
Rawdon! Rawdon, listen to me! Have we not both been fools? You knew the game and you let me play it! Where did we think it would end?

The men tumble to the landing below where Steyne slumps on the floor. Rawdon turns to his shaking wife.

RAWDON

Take off those things.

With fumbling hands, she starts to. But he cannot wait and snatching a diamond star from her bosom, he flings it down at Steyne, gashing him on the forehead.

RAWDON

Now get out!

Steyne snatches up the jewels and hurries down the stairs.

BECKY

Rawdon—

But he takes her wrist, dragging her into the drawing room.

INT. CURZON STREET HOUSE. DRAWING ROOM. NIGHT.
Rawdon pulls her over to the little desk.

RAWDON

Open it!

BECKY

But—

RAWDON

Open it! I want to see if he or you are lying!

She does not move. He wrenches it open. There, among the *billets doux* is the thousand pound note. Rawdon takes it up. Now he sounds sad more than angry.

RAWDON

A thousand pounds? You might have spared me a hundred, Becky. I always shared with you.

Crumpling the note in his hand, he throws it on the fire. They stare at each other. He starts down the staircase.

INT. CURZON STREET HOUSE. STAIRCASE AND HALL. NIGHT.
She follows him, increasingly desperate. He is at the door.

BECKY

Rawdon, forgive me, I made a grave mistake. I'm sorry. You cannot know the journey I have had to make.

RAWDON

I should. I travelled with you.

What? This isn't part of her plan. When he explains, his voice is quite gentle. They will not meet again on this earth and he does not wish to part from her in anger.

BECKY

Not from the beginning. Please, Rawdon, in my way I've loved you, I always will.

She does and he opens the door. Then he turns. She stands at the foot of the stair, still and magnificent. She has finished with begging. She looks him proudly in the eye.

But it is too late.

RAWDON

Then that is your misfortune. Goodbye, Rebecca.

The front door slams. She is alone.

INT. CURZON STREET HOUSE. DRAWING ROOM. DAY.
The footman, the butler and Raggles are sprawled around. They have raided Rawdon's cellars.

RAGGLES
This is a very fine port, gentlemen. Look at that colour.

FOOTMAN
Enjoy the colour of his port, why don't we? 'Cos we won't see the colour of his money!

In the coarse laugh that greets this, Becky steps into the doorway. She is astonished by what she sees.

BECKY
What are you thinking of? Simpson! Trotter! How dare you sit in my presence! Stand up at once or I'll turn you out!

FOOTMAN
Not without paying us, you won't.

BECKY
Mr Raggles, are you going to let them insult me?

RAGGLES
Oh Ma'am, I never thought it'd be a Crawley as would ruin me!

FOOTMAN
Get off your high horse and go and find us our wages.

BECKY
I will not be spoken to like this! When Colonel Crawley comes home—

This produces a loud, coarse laugh from the company. Only poor, swindled Raggles has still some sympathy for her.

RAGGLES
Beg pardon, Ma'am, but the Colonel ain't coming home. He's made that abundantly clear . . .

There it is. Becky is facing ruin.

INT. DRAWING ROOM. QUEEN'S CRAWLEY. DAY.
Rawdon is with Jane and Pitt who is reading from a newspaper.

PITT
"Following the premature death of His Excellency the Governor of Coventry Island, we hear the post is to be offered to Colonel Rawdon Crawley, the distinguished veteran of Waterloo." But this is excellent.

He gives the paper back to Rawdon.

RAWDON
Excellent be damned! The place is a graveyard and it is Steyne who sends me to it.

JANE
What? Why would he do that?

Both the men know why and they do not intend to discuss it.

PITT
Whatever the reason, it is a chance and you must take it.

RAWDON
I will take it. I am here to say goodbye. We will not meet again and so I hope we part in friendship but spare me your good wishes on my sunny tomb.

EXT. QUEEN'S CRAWLEY. DAY.
A groom holds Rawdon's horse. Pitt stands back as Jane kisses Rawdon's cheek in farewell.

RAWDON
Before I go, I must speak to you of Rawdy. In truth, it is why I have come but I cannot bear to talk of parting with him.

JANE
You cannot ask anything we will not grant. Please.

RAWDON
Then would you take care of him? Get him out of that damned school and give him a home? A proper home. My life has not been

much. Whatever I've touched has turned to dust. Except that boy. He is the best of me.

His voice is catching in his throat and he cannot continue.

JANE
Rawdon, I promise you faithfully, while I am alive I will love and cherish your son as if he were my own. I do already.

RAWDON
God bless you, my dearest Jane.

He takes her hand for a last time, mounts his horse and rides away down the drive. Pitt and Jane watch the stiff back of the soldier but we see his face where the tears flow freely.

EXT. COVENTRY ISLAND. DAY.
The sun burns down on the shanty town capital of Coventry Island. A rowing boat is docked at the quay. From it, walks Rawdon, in full regalia, plumed hat and uniform, his red face running with sweat. He is followed by a procession of humpers as he walks up the hill. He is watched by the inhabitants who laugh and talk dialect. As he stops, removes his hat, continues up the hill.

MAN (SUBTITLED)
He's big. Ten rupees that he lasts four years.

NEIGHBOR (SUBTITLED)
The big ones go quicker. He'll be dead in three.

They laugh as Rawdon walks on.

FADE

EXT. CRAWLEY HOUSE. DAY.
Becky, simply dressed, stands at the door of Crawley House. It is opened by Firkin, Miss Crawley's ancient lady's maid.

FIRKIN
What do you want?

BECKY
For God's sake, Firkin, where is Rawdy? The school writes that Lady Jane has taken him . . .

FIRKIN
And?

BECKY
I must see him—

FIRKIN

They're in the country.

Becky, desperate, cranes round her but Firkin stops her.

FIRKIN

*Leave him be, Mrs Crawley. Let there be one life that you
don't spoil. Just leave him be.*

*She shuts the door in Becky's face. After a moment, Becky turns and
walks away. If we ever doubted her love for her child, we see it now as
she walks on down the crowded street, oblivious of the tears that pour
down her cheeks.*

INT. GAMBLING CASINO. DAY.
Pumpernickel, Germany, 1833.

In a red-upholstered chamber, desperate men and dubious
women cluster round the tables. At one end is a buffet where the
gamblers may replenish their strength. Among the scoffing
grandees is a laughing group of young men. But as the camera
approaches we can see a woman in their midst in a shabby,
sequinned dress. She has just finished a story that makes them
howl with mirth. A young man reaches for a bottle of
Champagne to fill her glass. An official sees them and calls out.

OFFICIAL

Who will pay for that?

The woman looks down the line of diners, pointing.

WOMAN

Him, I think. Or him. Oh no, him. Definitely him.

She has found a particularly fat, rich-looking individual. The
official approaches the stranger.

We moved heaven and earth to have Tom Sturridge in the film.

He looked uncannily like Jonathan Rhys Meyers who plays his

father in the film—that same blazing beauty, petulance and

vanity in his face. —Mira Nair

OFFICIAL

She says you will pay for a bottle of Champagne.

STRANGER

Who? Who says that?

He follows the official's eye and finds the woman. She smiles a
dazzling smile beneath her mask.

WOMAN

You will, won't you? I am so *dreadfully* thirsty.

The young men watch in silence. But he is utterly beguiled.

STRANGER

Of course.

He raises his own glass in a toast. The official has been defeated.
The young men roar their approval. Across the room a croupier
motions to Becky that it is her turn to deal.

WOMAN

Hey, ho, off to work I go.

She rises and walks across to the gambling tables. Through the
door comes a proud fellow of eighteen. He drinks in everything
he sees. He stops at her table where she deals cards.

WOMAN

C'est votre premiere fois ici?

GEORGY

I'm afraid I don't—

WOMAN

Is this your first time in the Casino?

GEORGY

And if it is?

She laughs softly and disarms him.

WOMAN

Then you must use your Beginner's Luck wisely. The chance
will not come again.

DOBBIN

George!

Dobbin is hurrying through the tables towards them.

DOBBIN
What would Amelia say if she knew you were here?

George attempts to maintain his adult status.

GEORGE
Not now, Dobbin. Um . . . May I present Major Dobbin, a friend of my mother's? This is—

BECKY (FOR IT IS SHE)
But I know the Major very well.

Dobbin bows stiffly. He knows whom they are talking to.

DOBBIN
Mrs Crawley.

Georgy is amazed by this turn of events.

GEORGY
Don't tell me it is the infamous Mrs Crawley!

BECKY (COOLLY)
It is, Sir. So Amelia is travelling on the continent? Your grandfather forgave her in the end, then?

Dobbin shakes his head but Georgy answers anyway.

GEORGY
He did, God bless him. He left her well provided for.

BECKY
Alas, Major Dobbin, are you still only her "friend"?

Dobbin is affronted; Becky makes a decision.

BECKY
I should like to call on your mama while she is here.

GEORGY
You must! Come tomorrow. We are at the Erbprinz Hotel.

DOBBIN
But she won't want to be—

Becky is having none of this. She taps him with her fan.

BECKY
La, Major! I don't remember you for a tease! Tell her I'll be there in the morning.

She has started to leave when George's voice stops her.

GEORGY
You must have known my father. Do you think I am like him?

She pauses, thinking of that vain, long-dead popinjay.

BECKY
Very.

With a knowing look at her, Dobbin takes Georgy away. Dobbin is furious.

DOBBIN
George, it is not your place to issue invitations!

GEORGY
But if she's an old friend—

DOBBIN
She is an old *acquaintance*. It is not the same. Your mother won't wish to see her.

INT. ERBPRINZ HOTEL. AMELIA'S ROOM. DAY.
Amelia is twelve years older than when we met her last but still as pretty as ever. And as exasperating.

AMELIA
Of course I want to see her! Becky? How could I not?

DOBBIN
That little devil brings mischief wherever she goes. She killed her husband—

AMELIA
He died of tropical fever. You can hardly lay that at her door.

DOBBIN
Can't I?

Dobbin sighs with frustration. Amelia persists.

AMELIA
They took her son from her! Do you think I, of all people, would not sympathise with that?

DOBBIN
Rubbish! Rawdon took the boy away because cats are better mothers!

AMELIA
What do you know of motherhood! Or *fatherhood* for that matter! You have no child—

DOBBIN

Don't I know it! And if I have any authority in this house—

AMELIA

Authority? You have none, Sir! Who do you think you are? My father? My husband? *You are neither! And I will make my own decisions as to my behaviour!*

This has escalated into a full blown row but now, as her haughty words ring out, Dobbin looks at her. It is time. He has come to a resolution. His voice is become quite soft.

DOBBIN

You are right. I am not your husband nor ever likely to be.

She is silent, unsure as to quite what she has triggered.

DOBBIN

I know what your heart is capable of. It can cling faithfully to a misty memory and cherish a dream. But it cannot recognise or return a love like mine.

AMELIA

I have been your friend—

DOBBIN

No. You have allowed me to be *your* friend and I have bartered all my passion *for your little feeble remnant of affection. But I will bargain no more. I withdraw from the field.* Let this end. We are both weary of it.

AMELIA

You mean . . . you're going away?

DOBBIN

We have been prisoners, Amelia. You as much as I. If there is no future for us together, then let us see if we may each find one apart. We have spent enough of our lives at this play. Goodbye.

EXT. ERBPRINZ HOTEL. SPA CAFE DAY.

Amelia is pouring some tea for her visitor.

BECKY

When his cousin died, I knew Rawdy would spend his life at Queen's Crawley. Now Pitt is dead he is the Baronet. He belongs there.

AMELIA

But you must see him? Why don't you? Does Lady Jane prevent it?

BECKY

No. Jane would not keep me from him . . . But Rawdy has become a great man. I love him and I wish him well but my place is no longer with him.

Becky refuses to sink into melancholy and she is nearly ready to say what she's come for.

BECKY

Tell me how is Major Dobbin? I passed him as I came up looking very fierce.

AMELIA

We have fallen out.

BECKY

Over me? That's it, isn't it? He did not want you to see me. I could tell that when Georgy suggested it.

AMELIA

Over you, but over . . . other things as well.

BECKY

Amelia Osborne you are a damn fool! He is your dearest friend. It matters not what he thinks of me. Go and fetch him.

AMELIA

I cannot, Rebecca. You do not know how it stands between us.

BECKY

I do. Ever since I saw him buy that piano I've known how it stood.

AMELIA

What piano?

BECKY

The one he bought for you. At the auction of your father's possessions.

AMELIA

That was George.

171

BECKY

It was Dobbin. I saw him with my own eyes.

Amelia begins to digest this possibility.

AMELIA

That was George.

BECKY

Everyone knows it was Dobbin who persuaded George to defy his father and marry you.

AMELIA

He needed no persuasion. George loved me.

BECKY

George loved no one but himself. He'd have jilted you but for Dobbin and left you if he'd lived.

AMELIA

Stop! Silence! Dobbin was right! Wherever you go, you trail wickedness and heartache in your wake!

BECKY

I came prepared for this. George gave it to me at the Duchess of Richmond's Ball!

She has taken out an old, folded note. She proffers it.

AMELIA

I do not care what it is! I will not read it!

She jumps up but Becky holds her. She opens the paper.

BECKY

"My darling Becky, Won't you save me from a life of dreary toil? Fly with me. We will dance our way across Europe. Your George."

She looks into the eyes of her friend.

BECKY

That is the man you have made your life a shrine to.

Becky releases Amelia's arm but she is completely still. She takes the paper from Becky's hand and stares at it.

AMELIA

I have been a fool.

BECKY

We have all been fools. But you may still remedy your folly.

There is a noise in the courtyard below. From the window they can see Dobbin supervising the loading of his baggage.

BECKY

Hurry.

Amelia runs to the door. Then she stops.

AMELIA

Becky, I do not know if you are a kind person—

BECKY

I'm not.

AMELIA

But you have always been kind to me. Always. Why?

BECKY

You know me, you know my weaknesses. I have always courted the great world. Perhaps I was blinded by vanity and ambition. When I could see again, I had lost everyone I ever loved and I cannot let you make the same mistake. Go! Now! Before you waste the next twenty years as well!

EXT. ERBPRINZ HOTEL. DAY.

Amelia appears and runs towards Dobbin who is watching as the last of his things are loaded. She speaks and he spins in surprise. With barely a word more, they fly into each other's arms.

INT. CASINO. DAY

The gaming room is once more in action with gamblers, desperate and dilettante, leaning on the tables. Becky enters. The sit of her head and the sag of her shoulders tell us that the world lies heavily upon her. One of her young admirers approaches.

YOUNG MAN

Angel Englanderinn! Take compassion upon us. Dine with Fritz and me at the inn in the park. We'll die if you don't.

BECKY

Tomorrow, maybe. Ask me again tomorrow. Tonight I'm a little . . . tired.

He wonders at her mood as she walks on, sinking at last against a table. She raises her hand and lets her face fall forward into it.

She is very, very low.

JOSEPH (V.O.)
I am looking for a Madame de Crawley. Can you tell me where I might find her?

Becky's fingers open revealing her eyes. She looks over. Sure enough, it is Joseph Sedley placing a bet.

BECKY
Mr Sedley? Mr Joseph Sedley?

Jos looks up. He cannot quite make her out at first.

JOSEPH
By Jove! Have I found you? Amelia said you were here. Is it truly the beautiful Mrs Crawley?

BECKY
Beautiful? I don't know about that but it is Mrs Crawley. Or should I say the Widow Crawley for that is my name now . . .

JOSEPH
Yes. Ahem. Most sorry to hear about it. A fine man and all that . . .

BECKY
I see you are at the tables, you must be a brilliant player knowing the relish with which you have embraced danger and risk in your life. You still haven't told me what you're doing here.

JOSEPH
I have stared down my share of elephants, but all that is past. It's time to enjoy my fortune now. I'm on my way back to India.

Becky's eyes light up like a greyhound's at the sight of the rabbit.

BECKY
India?

EXT. PUMPERNICKEL HOTEL. DAY
The luggage is being loaded. Joseph and Becky are in travelling clothes. He hands her up into the carriage.

JOSEPH
By Gad, Mrs Crawley, what a turn up! I do hope the travelling will not tire you?

She gives him a beaming smile.

BECKY
Oh no, Mr Sedley! You know that I love to visit new places.

And she falls back with him against the cushions, laughing with glee at the start of her next adventure. As the carriage moves off, the camera slides over their heads and down the back of the vehicle. There, roped to the fender, is the old, battered trunk with its initial, R.S. The very trunk that has followed its mistress so faithfully through all of her journeys . . . .

THE END.

Ah! *Vanitas Vanitatum!* Which of us is happy in this world? Which of us has his desire? Or, having it, is satisfied?—come, children, let us shut up the box and the puppets, for our play is played out.

—William Makepeace Thackeray, *Vanity Fair,* 1847